The Guns of Frank Eaton

David Althouse

WHEELER PUBLISHING
A part of Gale, a Cengage Company

Farmington Hills, Mich • San Francisco • New York • Waterville, Maine
Meriden, Conn • Mason, Ohio • Chicago

Wheeler Publishing, a part of Gale, a Cengage Company.

Wheeler Publishing Large Print Western.
The text of this Large Print edition is unabridged.
Other aspects of the book may vary from the original edition.
Set in 16 pt. Plantin.

LIBRARY OF CONGRESS CIP DATA ON FILE.
CATALOGUING IN PUBLICATION FOR THIS BOOK
IS AVAILABLE FROM THE LIBRARY OF CONGRESS

ISBN-13: 978-1-4328-6068-4 (softcover)

Published in 2019 by arrangement with Wolfpack Publishing

Printed in Mexico
1 2 3 4 5 6 7 23 22 21 20 19

To DeWayne "Poppy" Luster,
veteran of the Second World War
who fought in the Philippines and
whose many firsthand stories of
Frank "Pistol Pete" Eaton serve as
the inspiration for this novel.

1

"I don't have much longer to go, and I'll soon learn what waits for me beyond the veil, so I don't have any reason to tell you anything but the truth, hear?"

I will never forget those words from Frank "Pistol Pete" Eaton. That statement introduced me to a story told in his own words, a story of love and revenge that sprawled across an untamed frontier during a time when men skinned their own hides and evened their own scores. Those introductory words assured me that the words I was about to hear were as true as the water that flowed down the nearby Cimarron.

Growing up in early day Oklahoma, I heard my fair share of tales out of the Old West, often times straight from the men who lived them.

Oklahoma joined the Union on November 16, 1907. Up until that time, the region had stood mostly as lawless and wide-open country, a land of small mountain ranges, prairie, mesas, and eastern forests roamed by American Indians, cowboys, outlaws, hardened peace officers, and adventurers of all sorts. Many of those grizzled men of the frontier lived long into the 1900's, a rare few into the 1950's, and their thrilling stories demanded folks listen in rapt attention.

I heard stories told down through the ages dating back to the time of the great Spanish conquistadores and the treasure those early explorers buried in the Wichita Mountain range of southern Oklahoma.

I listened as folks told of Jesse and Frank James who, in December of 1875, journeyed into the Mexican state of Chihuahua where they successfully attacked and robbed a burro train hauling gold bullion worth an estimated two million dollars. The outlaw band made their escape northward across the state of Texas to the Wichita Mountains of present-day Oklahoma and, while waiting out a late winter storm in March of 1876, buried the loot in a gulch and then caved in the ravine's sides so as to cover the treasure to this very day.

Oklahoma possessed outlaws in great quantity, so the stories never ended of their many colorful adventures across the region.

There was the Doolin Gang, Ned Christie, Belle Starr, Henry Starr, the Dalton Boys, The Buck Gang and the Martin Boys.

Accounts of the famous Doolin Gang loomed large during my upbringing. Bill Doolin ran the gang, the notorious Wild Bunch, robbing banks and stores, holding up trains, and killing officers all across Indian Territory, Kansas, Arkansas and Missouri. At the young age of thirty-eight, Doolin met his violent end in Lawson, Oklahoma Territory in the fall of 1896.

The list of cutthroats in the Indian Territory who killed for pleasure ran long. It included wanton killers such as Cherokee Bill, Ned Christie, Smoker Mankiller, John Billee and Blue Duck. There were rapists such as Martin Joseph and Jason Labreu. To boot, there were simple looters like Jim French, Bob Rogers, and the Cook Gang.

When it comes to cowboy stories, Oklahoma owns them in abundance. The famous Chisholm Trail runs straight through the middle of the state and its now dim trace keeps the secrets of scores of drovers who pushed longhorns from deep in Texas to the Kansas railheads during a twenty-two-year period beginning in 1867.

Oklahoma gave birth to the Pawnee Bill Wild West Show and the 101 Real Wild West

Show, two over-the-top Wild West extravaganzas that took the story of America's Western frontier around the world. These Wild West shows often employed performers who had lived the wild and woolly life in old Indian Territory, cowboys and cowgirls such as Will Rogers and Lucille Mulhall.

Such history is a reminder of Oklahoma's pivotal role in creating the great American cowboy.

To understand the story of Frank Eaton — gunfighter, lawman, cowboy, and rodeo performer — one must understand how held over animosities from the War Between the States helped determine the affairs of men in Indian Territory, Kansas and Texas following that great fracas.

The war produced hardened men from both sides, and those that poured into the border regions after 1865 met with — and helped give name to — the Wild West.

When battle-honed, yet enterprising Confederate Texans returned home after the war, they found their state ravaged by the effects of that four-year-long conflict. They found an answer to the economic turmoil in the roaming Longhorn cattle that had fattened, matured, and multiplied to an estimated five million strong while able bodied

Texans had fought. Thus began the historic cattle drives from Texas, via the aforementioned Chisholm Trail through Indian Territory to the Kansas railheads. Wild, wide-open and vice-filled cow towns quickly sprang up all along the thoroughfare, offering heavily armed and rambunctious cowhands every opportunity to part with their recent earnings. Rustling, robberies, and wanton murder ran rampant, often times manifested along North-South lines. Texas became a hotbed of violence between ex-Confederate Texans and the Carpetbaggers new to the state. Eastern Kansas simmered with post-war tension and children watched as their parents fell to the gun. Indian Territory — now the state of Oklahoma — became the most lawless, the most incredibly violent region in the history of the American West, the one region without law, a cauldron of crime for the new soldiers of fortune of the frontier — the horse and cattle thief, the prostitute, the whisky peddler, the desperado. Men killed over such issues as the ownership of boots.

In the entire Western frontier, no region loomed as dangerous to the badged officer as Indian Territory. Little wonder the future state of Oklahoma produced for the ages numerous men considered quintessential

Western lawmen — men such as Bill Tilghman, Bass Reeves and Heck Thomas.

The type of men who crisscrossed this violent country made up a who's who of Old West gunfighters — men such as the James Boys, the Dalton Gang, Ned Christie, Sam Bass, Wild Bill Hickok, and Frank Eaton. Many of these men were fighting veterans of the War Between the States, men from both North and South, men whose life experiences tilted their allegiance to only one law — the law of the gun. The most violent of these, consisting of men still stinging with the bitterness of defeat at the hands of the Yankees, was a band of murderous criminals known as the Regulators.

The Regulators commenced their lawless activities in southeastern Kansas in the years immediately after the war. When the heat of the law became too hot to handle in Kansas, the Regulators relocated south to the Indian Territory, a region scarce of men wearing badges. Once firmly entrenched in the Indian Territory their numbers grew upwards to approximately sixty men, each of them hardened criminals. Their network spread far and wide, north to Missouri and Kansas with small fragments of their numbers reaching as far west as New Mexico.

I cannot remember the first time I laid

eyes on Frank Eaton, but he enjoyed legend status in my hometown of Perkins, Oklahoma and beyond. He owned and worked a blacksmith shop in town and occasionally dug new water wells and helped clear old ones that had collapsed. These were old world skills but still much in demand in rural Oklahoma even up into the 1950's, the period from which I remember him best. He sported long braided hair underneath a ten-gallon Western sombrero, wore holstered sidearms, and donned a thick mustache across a leather-like face — quite a spectacle in the 1950's, especially to a young and curious boy like me. After all, a great world war had ended only a few years earlier, the Cold War raged in full swing, airplanes darted across the sky and men worked in earnest on the world's first artificial satellite.

Yet, in Perkins, Oklahoma, there walked a living, breathing artifact straight out of the Wild West. While youngsters across the country watched Roy Rogers and Gene Autry at the Saturday matinee to get their taste of the old days on the American frontier, I just had to walk downtown. Locals often asked him to tell stories and he always obliged. Sometimes out-of-towners rolled into town asking for him by name. They, too, asked to hear his yarns and to witness his firearms skills. Frank eagerly obliged. The loud booms of his period sidearms interrupted many otherwise quiet afternoons during my upbringing.

Sometimes he set up matchsticks at a goodly distance as targets. He backed up a respectable number of steps then began firing, shooting first with one hand and then with another in a steady cadence of gunfire. He never missed.

Other times he chose a metal bucket as his target, slinging the pail down the middle of Main Street before firing away in alternating fashion with both sidearms. Many times the bucket became airborne, and a steady stream of dead shots kept it from falling before Frank had emptied his weapons. Again, he never missed.

At first, the reasons for his popularity were unknown to me. I asked my mother about the colorful relic's background, and I remember her words to this day: "Never mind about that crazy old man! He's a murderer and I want you to stay away from him. Hear?" Several times, upon hearing my mother's words against Frank, my father broke in to assure that the old gunman posed no threat to anyone, at least not in modern times, as the objects of his deadly shooting skills had long since passed over the great divide in dramatic fashion.

Naturally, I wanted to learn everything possible about the old man. My time came one day while on a trip to town with my mother.

As we strode up to the mercantile in which my mother had business to conduct, we saw a crowd gathered around Frank listening to one of his stories. Frank possessed a booming voice and his words carried throughout downtown Perkins.

Mother approached the wood steps to the mercantile where I let go of her hand and began darting after Frank. She fathomed my intentions at once and called after me.

"Stay away from that old man, Jesse!"

"I want to talk with him, mother."

"Stay away from him, hear? That old man was an outlaw."

"That's Frank Eaton. I want to hear his stories."

"Don't go near him, hear?"

"But dad knows him and likes him."

"That's your father's view, but it isn't mine. Stay away from that ol' murderer until I'm done in town. Once I'm done here then I'm off to the parlor. I'll be awhile so wait here."

"Murderer?"

"That's what I said."

Mother gave me a disapproving stare and then entered the mercantile. By this time, Frank had finished with his story and had gone back to his blacksmith shop a short distance away.

I ran down the street to Frank's blacksmith at a fast clip. Once there, I pulled the creaky, loosely hinged door open and beheld once again the old man. He stood near a pit of hot coals, using blacksmith's tongs to hold a horseshoe. His was a ramshackle enterprise lit only by the sunlight penetrating through the cracks and gaps in the board walls. Not taking his eyes away from his work, he recognized my presence.

"You make a habit of following men unawares, boy?"

I stood motionless, unable to mutter a syllable. I looked up in awe at the old rock statue of a man adorned in wide-brim hat and sporting six-guns at each side. A few awkward seconds went by before I whispered my first words.

"Are you a murderer?"

"Some folks may think I am, but people don't always want to hear the truth, boy."

"What do you mean?"

"There's a few don't believe my stories as it is, and maybe I don't tell everything.

They'd really think me crazy if I told the unvarnished accounts."

"What do you mean by unvarnished?"

"What's your name, boy?"

"Jesse, Jesse Stamper."

"Know your father. Also knew your grandfather. Dug a well for him a long time ago. Where's your mother? Didn't I just see you with her a few minutes ago?"

"She's at the mercantile and then down to the parlor. Won't be out for probably hours. Please, will you tell me your story?"

"Hours, you say? Boy, you don't want to get caught with me. As you say, I'm known as a murderer by some hereabouts."

"I hear folks say that. But I don't know if I believe them, and I don't care if they're true, anyway."

"It's my label to some."

"Why?"

"Surprised you haven't heard of it. Made a name for myself years back when I set out to avenge the murder of my father."

"Who murdered your father?"

"Outfit what called itself the Regulators up in Kansas. Started out a small group, but grew. Murdered my father in cold blood, shot him down like a mad dog."

"You went after them?"

"It was a job needed doin'."

"What happened?"

"Opened up a hornets' nest. By the time I grew up and started on their trail the small group of six or seven who murdered father had grown to a murderin' gang of about sixty hate-filled rattlesnakes. But I didn't know that when I killed the first one."

My interest grew with each word uttered by the old, stoned-faced man. I stood with my eyes transfixed on his every word, his every move.

"And yet you're still here. I wanna know what happened. How'd you take on so many men?"

"Part of it was luck. That, and I had the advantage of geography, some say."

"I don't understand."

"What I mean is I squared off with 'em in a place where the lay of the land played to my advantage."

"Where was that?"

"Out in that beautiful mesa country of eastern New Mexico. Turns out a man afoot and leaving no tracks can be an almost even match for a passel of murderin' coyotes beholdin' to their horses in that country."

Frank stirred the coals in the fire pit and the red light reflected on his face as he looked contemplatively into the cauldron of light. *What secrets he must safeguard be-*

neath that braided hair and humongous ten-gallon hat, I thought.

"Them sonsabitches trailed me out to that country whilst I trailed the last of the original six."

"The last of the original six means you got the first five, right?"

"Hold on, boy. It's not safe to make assumptions, especially when you're up against a first-rate gang of cutthroats like the Regulators. And, leastways, a man most often doesn't get everything he wants."

"I'll quit interrupting, sir."

"I looked over that wonderful mesa land and concocted a plan. Right as I found myself all alone in that great, wide-open country it came to me all to once. I had to get rid of my horse."

"You gave up your horse? Who does such a thing? What was his name?"

"Folks called him Bowlegs. I called him Bo for short. He was a beautiful Paint."

"Never heard of someone giving up a good horse. Mr. Eaton, you just gotta tell the whole thing, everything from start to finish. Please?"

"You believe in curses, boy? You believe a man's life can be lived out on a damned dark spell?"

If the old man didn't have my attention to

that point, he surely gained it then.

"What do you mean by a spell?"

Frank set down his tongs, pulled up two wooden stools and arranged them side by side.

"Alright, boy let's set for a bit. What I'm going to tell you is the story from beginning to end. She's an unvarnished story, but she's as true as the North Star on a cold winter night in the mountains. I don't have much longer to go, and I'll soon learn what awaits for me beyond the veil, so I don't have any reason to tell you anything but the truth, savvy?"

"Yes, sir."

"Now, after I'm gone, you can repeat my story if you're of a mind to. Just know some people may think we're both crazy — me for telling it and you for believing it enough to repeat it. I'll be long gone and won't care a damn."

My name is Jesse Stamper of Perkins, Oklahoma, home of Frank "Pistol Pete" Eaton, and the account I lay before you now is the exact story the old gunfighter recited to me on a chill fall day in his blacksmith shop next to the fire many years ago.

2

I said a spell and that's what I mean, but you're not going to understand until I back up a bit and start from the beginning.

It all started many years ago, right after the great War Between the States when I was about your age, growing up in southeast Kansas along the Santa Fe Trail.

All things considered, living along the Santa Fe Trail shouldn't have been too bad of a thing for a young boy. Stories of the trail most always conjured up visions of the Spanish conquistadors, mountain men, explorers, frontiersmen and traders what had traipsed along it for many years.

The trail started in Independence, Missouri and ran all the way southwest across the country to Santa Fe in what is now New Mexico.

Folks had often spoke of that early Spanish conquistador, Coronado, who brought a party of men over what is now the Oklahoma panhandle back in the 1500's. Folks talked about how those conquistadores most surely had covered that area of the panhandle where the Santa Fe Trail crosses.

People around home spoke of the many dangers that sections of the trail offered up to even the most hardened of frontiersmen down through the many years of its history.

Take Jedediah Strong Smith, for example. He was one of our country's foremost mountain men. In those early days of our country, Smith wandered all over the place and encountered all kinds of travails, hair-raising dangers from which he was damned lucky to escape. He had traveled up the Missouri River for furs. He had explored the Black Hills region of the Dakotas where he survived the mauling of a grizzly bear. He led the first expedition across the Southwest to California. He explored the Great Salt Lake and helped to identify what eventually became known as "South Pass," which was easy route through the Rocky Mountains.

Smith had done all of those things and lived to tell the stories. But after his days of exploring were over, Smith decided to enter what he thought would be the less-dangerous mercantile business.

That decision cost him his life one day as

he traveled along the Santa Fe Trail.

It was about 1831 and he was traipsing along the Kansas side of the dangerous Cimarron Cutoff section of the trail when he was overwhelmed and killed by a band of Comanche Indians. Smith was as seasoned as they came, a tough hombre, but he didn't make it on his very first attempt to cross the famous route. He was just thirty-two years of age, tough and in his prime.

My upbringing gave me to know of many others who met early ends along that trail. Father brought mother and me to our new home by the trail in the years right after the great War Between the States. That was a period in which many people used the trail to leave that troubled region of the country to the east where much of the war had happened. We saw many wagonloads of folks traveling westward over the years, and wherever there are people there is almost always trouble. Bands of robbers saw the travelers as easy pickings. These bands often robbed travelers of their few possessions and treasure and rustled their cattle.

Our little part of the world that sat near that historic trail was a region boiled over with violence between Northern Vigilantes and Southern Regulators, men still fighting the war even after Lee's surrender at Appomattox, and both sides had hired gunmen. Father was leader of the Northern faction and was always courting trouble and threats on his life. Those Regulators hated him.

Father, about thirty-five years old at the time, stood six feet tall, had kind brown eyes, dark brown hair and a heavy mustache. While tolerant of others and respectful of other opinions, he was a man of strong convictions and was a hard man to turn when it came to matters of right and wrong. He was never quarrelsome, but when someone pushed him to the limit he owned a violent temper and you had better draw distance and let the Good Lord supply the lightning rods.

The Regulators were led by a man named Si Dodder. Dodder was a man what liked to steal horses and cattle from the emigrant trains along the Santa Fe Trail. He would hide them and then later collect a reward for finding them.

Some say he learned his crafty, thieving ways from descendants of the Murrell Gang, the infamous band of outlaws and cutthroats from out of the Old South led by John Murrell. Murrell was best known as a land pirate, working all along the Mississippi River in those early days of the 1800's. Murrell's specialty was stealing and then reselling slaves, stealing cattle and general gut robbing and highway banditry.

Murrell and his band often stole slaves and cattle from folks throughout the South just to collect the eventual reward money. In order to identify themselves to one another, members of the Murrell Gang had a black locust tree bordered by two Spanish dagger plants in their front yards. Another way of identification was by wearing a certain gold medallion around their necks. It was a vast network of criminals, as the stories go, and included members who masqueraded as honorable and legitimate men during the light of day. The Murrell Gang was a real secret society, a dark and cutthroat crowd using code words, secret handshakes and symbols to operate without fear of discovery.

Them Regulators did the same kind of thing. They stole cattle from folks traveling westward along the trail, held the cattle for a spell, then resold the same livestock to folks what traveled along the same trail a month later. They liked to wear boots with the high-shafts painted up with tarot card images, most notably devil and death, as identification.

Leastways, father and his northern friends said they had it on good authority at the time that these Regulators had some kind of link to folks connected to that early-day Murrell Gang.

Right under Dodder in the Regulator chain of command were six men from the nearby Campsey and Ferber families. We didn't see much of Dodder but them Campseys and Ferbers caused us all kinds of trouble for the folks thereabouts. Sonsabitches is what they were!

Seems like those Regulators was always in a fracas of some kind — killing someone at a poker or faro table, killing someone who called them out on their cattle rustling, or killing an innocent Indian who happened to cross paths with one or more of the band on a trail somewhere. They robbed banks in Kansas and Missouri and they would kill at the drop of a hat. They hated Yankees and anything that resembled one. They believed that law and order was a joke in light of injustices done against them and theirs during and after the war.

Now, don't get me wrong. There were hired guns on both sides — the Vigilantes had them and so did the Regulators. And there was bad men on both sides. It's just that those Regulators had mastered a special kind of ornery meanness.

Like I said before, you could always tell them sonsabitches by the clothes they wore. Most of them wore high shaft boots decorated with devil and death tarot cards. They wore silver buckles, colorful sashes and some of them had gold teeth. One of them wore a black patch over his eye. Leastways, what I'm trying to say is they carried themselves kind of flashy and you could always tell when one or more of them bastards stood in your midst.

If you ever read about pirates on the high seas and thought about how they must've looked, then think about that stirred in with the frontier dress of the day. That's what a Regulator looked like.

If there was something I wasn't into as a young boy then it wasn't worth getting into. Trouble courted me just as it did my father. And, if trouble didn't find me then I went looking for it.

I'd a passion for them gypsies what traveled along the Santa Fe Trail back in those days. Father's farm and boarding house set on a hill right above the trail, and every time I saw one of those gypsy vardos passing along I made a beeline for it. I loved to have them gypsy womenfolk read me the tarot cards or look into the ball and give me their mysterious divinations.

Sometimes they'd go to playing their music and everyone would go to dancing and having a grand time. I couldn't help but to join in the dancing what with all of those fiddle and guitar players playing that fast-paced music. Them gypsies know how to have a good time.

They also know how to cook! I sat at many o' gypsy table and never went away hungry.

I'll tell you something else — I loved sitting in the midst of them beautiful, dark-eyed, raven-haired gypsy women, young and old alike. Even as a young boy about eight years old, they had me charmed with their mysterious looks and ways. I loved to dance with them and hear them sing. I loved to watch as they moved to-and-fro around the camp singing their little singsong ditties. They were unlike any of the womenfolk of southeast Kansas that I knew of and I just couldn't resist them.

Them gypsies was a spot of fun and happiness in a world made sorrowful by all of that animosity from the war — a war that was still being fought between Northerners and Southerners in our neck of the woods called southeast Kansas.

Like I said before, in those early days, when I was just a kid of a boy, there were six of them Regulator bastards who caused a good part of the trouble. There was Shannon Campsey, the leader, wearing a goatee and thick mustache swirled at the ends. Shannon had three brothers who rode with him — Jim, Jonce and Wyley. Then there was Doc and John Ferber. Shannon ruled with an iron fist and his brothers, as well as the two Ferber brothers, rode loyal.

Shannon and Wyley must've lived with all kinds of stored up rage and hatred for folks. Shannon was known thereabouts as a special kind of devil, a mean rattlesnake. To boot, his brother Wyley was feared most of all. Wyley was known to be a top-notch gun artist in that country and folks got goose bumps at the mention of his name.

They fancied themselves mighty high in those days, riding around the countryside bedecked in broad-brim hats, silver-studded belts and gun leather, swords, and high boots decorated with devil and death tarot cards. They rode on the best mounts, not settling for the typical jug-headed farm horses. No sir, they rode high and mighty in all their fancy trappings. Many folks shivered in fear when these hellhounds rode up. I was scared to death of them back when I was a kid of a boy.

One day, father and I went to town on

business. Father and I were standing inside the Osage County Savings and Loan when the six Regulators wrapped reins outside and barged hell-for-leather into the bank. Father and I had already been to the bank teller counter and had conducted our business. Father stood talking with a friend whilst I waited.

Shannon was the first through the door and he immediately cast his attention upon the four tellers behind the wooden bars of the bank's counter.

"Swing your partners, boys and ladies to the center! Well now, look here, Wyley. These boys look itchy. You four behind the counter there, no need to act antsy. You got those wood bars betwixt you and us."

I remember thinking the four tellers looked scared to death as they faced these murdering bastards. The head teller, if such he was, mustered out a few words of greeting in his northern accent.

"Who are you, sir? And what is your business here?"

"Hear that, Wyley? I told you this was a Yankee bank. Maybe we want to make a deposit. Let me ask you. Who are you and where are you from?"

"The name is Greenly. From Ohio."

"The hell you say, sir! So you decided to

move to Kansas?"

"I have a place in Ohio, too. What business do you . . ."

"Well isn't that nice, sir. I'm from Missouri. Use to have a place there. I don't have any place now."

"Very sorry . . ."

"I'm sure you're very sorry, sir. My place was lost because I didn't pay taxes on it while I was off fightin' you flat-headed, blue-bellied sonsabitches! Now there is a Yankee plowin' my fields, right Wyley?"

"Sir, please state your business here."

"We'll get to that right soon. Yep, Greenly, that's what I came home to — a farm that was no longer mine. I couldn't farm. Couldn't run for office. Couldn't teach. Couldn't preach. Couldn't even vote."

"I must caution you we have law in this town."

"Isn't that nice. You know, before the war, I was a lawman. One of the best. Now they say I live outside the law. Funny thing, the law."

"So you're here to rob this bank?"

"We don't like to call it robbin'. We like to call it appropriatin'."

All to once, them banker men behind the wood bars went for the guns they had concealed behind the counter. Poor bastards. Before they could even get their guns to bear their bodies were riddled with bullet holes to a man. Their bodies crumpled onto the floor where they lay in their own blood. I had never seen such an evil, gruesome act in my life and the picture of it all remains with me to this day.

Whilst all of this went on, father threw himself atop me to shield me from any gunfire. Wyley Campsey, the evil snake that he was, took notice.

"Look here, Shannon! That's old man Eaton, head Vigilante, along with his boy. Whataya say we finish this horseshit right here, right now?"

"Leave 'em be."

Loyal as he was to his brother, I could see on Wyley's face he sure wanted to kill father and me that day. Instead, Wyley fired a round into father's leg. Father wanted to scream, I know, but he just grit his teeth and grimaced. Then, Wyley pulled father from atop me and looked me square in the eyes.

That Wyley was an evil bastard. Shannon yelled at Wyley, asking what in the hell was he doing.

"It's time to finish them both and that includes his Yankee spawn."

Wyley took aim, pointing his sidearm barrel right between my eyes. Shannon ran over to Wyley and pulled him away from me. I was terrified.

As them six bastards got near the door to leave, Wyley turned around and directed words straight at me.

"I'm gettin' you one day, boy! Don't you ever forget it."

Shannon yanked Wyley through the front door of that bank and that passel of murdering sonsabitches stormed out onto the boardwalk, mounted their horses and stormed away. I still hear the thundering hooves of their horses as they rode off, and I still hear Wyley's words, "I'm gettin' you one day, boy! Don't you ever forget it."

3

Those words haunted me for years in the worst kind of way, and they still sometimes echo against the walls of my memory to this day.

Father walked with a severe limp from that point on. To this day, I remember how father put his life on the line to save mine. Father loved mother and me and wanted only the best for us. Oftentimes, my mind takes me back to one of my last moments alone with father. There was an ancient cottonwood what stood about a hundred yards from our farm, and father and me sat beneath its shade many times talking about any manner of things. It's all like a hazy dream now, but I remember I'd been some overcome by that incident at the bank and was worried about father.

"You're going to walk with a bad limp, father, all the days of your life for protecting me."

"In hindsight, Wyley Campsey was gonna put a bullet into me regardless. His brother'd killed me had he wanted, and he may do it yet. They know I'll not rest until this country is free of those murderin' skunks."

"Maybe we should just leave here like mother wants."

"Not even gonna think about that. Worked too hard for it and its all we got. One day it's yours."

Now, I have to tell you something. Never once growing up did I see myself as a farmer like father. That was his dream for me, but it wasn't my dream for myself. At the time, I didn't know what I'd do with my life, but I knew I wasn't interested in farming. But I never told father anything such.

"Mine, father?"

"Yours if you want it. That's another reason we have to defeat them bastards — to make this country safe for law and order folks. Don't run, son. It becomes a habit."

"I hate them Regulators, father."

"Don't ever run from their like. I hope you will carry on what we started here. Our boarding house will keep getting more business as traveling along the trail increases, and you'll always have the farm."

The sun dropped lower on the horizon

and a sort of reddish color lit up the western sky as we sat amidst the black shadow underneath that old cottonwood tree. Father had a lot to say that evening.

"Always been a fighter when it got right down to it. Any son of mine will be the same. Could be you're gonna be better at it than me. Leastways, promise me you'll never take it from any man, hear?"

"I give you my word, father."

"Something else I've been wanting to talk with you about, son."

"Yes, sir.'

"You've been seeing those gypsies what travel along the trail down there, haven't you?"

I hesitated.

"Don't lie to me, son."

"Yes, sir."

"I know you're charmed by their divinations, conjurings and the like. You know we don't hold with such, right, son?"

"I do, father."

"You're young, full of life, I suppose. You want the strange and mysterious, but I wish you'd learn to love the God-fearin', simple life we have here."

I looked off toward that fire red horizon, but didn't answer. All I could think of was Wyley Campsey's words to me. Those words kept repeating in my mind. "I'm gettin' you one day, boy! Don't you ever forget it."

Soon after the bank shootout, there came another day I'll never forget.

Father was away at a Vigilante meeting and mother was working in the house while I tended to livestock on our farm. Whilst working, I looked down to the trail and spied three colorful gypsy vardos ambling on to the westward. No sooner had I started sprinting off down the hill to the gypsy vardos than the stern voice of my mother reached my ears.

"Stop, Frank! Get back here! It's the woodshed again if your father hears you've been with gypsies again! Frank!"

It was no use. Like I said before, I was drawn to them gypsies like night bugs to a campfire. I was an ornery kid, truth be told, and mother just turned and went back in the house once she saw I weren't answering her plea.

Once I got down to the trail, I hailed the caravan to a stop. There was an elderly fellow atop the lead vardo and he brought the whole shindig to a stop when he saw me. The two other vardos behind him also stopped and assorted folks started pouring out of the colorful wagons.

These were gypsies I had never seen before.

I asked the lead driver about getting my fortune read and he just motioned me to the rear door of his vardo. I then stepped up on the small rear ladder of the head vardo and knocked on the door.

The door opened and I peered in to behold a young girl looking to be about the same age as me. Boy, was she beautiful! I had never seen such a girl as her! I was awe struck by her olive colored skin, by her raven black hair and by her equally dark eyes. She wore a colorful dress that topped everything off and I was in her corner from then on and forever more!

Inside the vardo was all kinds of things I never saw anywhere else. There were crystals, books, tarot cards, and colorful candles. Also sitting inside was an elderly woman and a young boy who looked to be about the same age as me. I directed my gaze to the elderly woman.

"Ma'am, will you read me the cards?"

The old woman gave me a fearful look that I didn't understand, like she was looking right through me, like she already knew my fortune with or without the use of any tarot cards.

"Are you sure your folks want you visiting

here, boy? We're gypsies and they may not want you mingling with our kind."

"Father is away and mother is cooking."

"Is that your house at the top of the hill?"

"It's ours. Father's at a meeting of the Vigilantes."

"What are Vigilantes?"

"They want to put a stop to the southern Regulators hereabouts. Them killers."

"The same gang robbing wagons along the trail?"

"That's them."

"We heard of them when we came through here last year."

"Father is top dog Vigilante. Them Regulators have rustled our cattle and our friends' cattle."

About that time the elderly lady looked to the beautiful young girl I was so stricken with.

"Adelita, this boy looks to be equal in years with you. Would you like to read him the cards?"

"Yes, grandmother."

I couldn't take my eyes off the girl. I'm telling you right now, she was a sparkler. I had to find out everything I could about her.

"What's your name?"

"I'm Adelita."

"I'm Frank, Frank Eaton."

I looked over to the young boy who looked to be the same age as Adelita and me.

"What's your name?"

The boy didn't answer, so Adelita answered for him.

"His name is Stevo. He's my cousin."

Adelita reached into a drawer by the table and took out a deck of tarot cards wrapped in a scarf dazzling with color, a scarf nearly one yard square, all lit up with colors of turquoise, red, and purple colored flowers against a bright orange background. She removed the cards from inside the scarf and began shuffling the deck. I was amazed at how she skillfully dealt with them cards. I had seen father play poker and faro with men from the area and Adelita's little hands worked them cards just as good as any of father's friends. I kept taking more of a liking to her.

Then, she commenced talking and I fell for her even more.

"These are my very own cards. My grandmother taught me how to use them. She gave me the scarf, too."

"Are these cards accurate? I snuck down here to the trail before and was read to by a woman using what looked like a glass ball. Nothing came of it."

"Grandmother says the cards are always right. Right, grandmother?"

"Just read the boy his cards, child."

About that time, Adelita told me to place my hands on the cards and I did so, leaving my hands atop them for several moments. Adelita then picked up the deck again, shuffled, cut, and laid the cards face down on the table. From the facedown deck, she began turning the cards over to reveal what they were. She laid down the Nine of Swords, the Ten of Swords, the Ace of Swords, the Devil, and then Death. I was some concerned.

"What in hell do those mean?"

"The Nine of Swords represents great turmoil, the Ten of Swords great cruelty, the Ace of Swords a sudden loss of something you love."

"But what about those other cards?"

Adelita's grandmother never let her answer.

"That's enough, Adelita. Your mother looks for you, boy. Now, go."

"But she has two more cards to tell me about."

"No matter. You must go."

Well, I was damned disappointed because I didn't want to leave that beautiful Adelita and I also wanted to hear the rest of what she had to say about the cards. I got the feeling that maybe her grandmother was trying to protect me, and maybe also trying to protect Adelita, but from what I had no idea. I still remember the concerned look on the grandmother's face and the way she cut things off all to once. As I got up from my chair, the grandmother made the sign of the cross and began mumbling something in a language I did not understand. Years later, I heard someone else utter those same words and learned they made up a special Catholic protection prayer said in Latin. Anyways, I climbed out the back of the vardo and began running up the hill to the house. I turned to look back at the vardo one more time and the grandmother was still making the sign of the cross as she watched me go.

4

I will never forget the details of what happened later that night. It was a night what started with a passel of bad premonitions on my part, deep down gut feelings that gave me to fear what might be coming.

After supper, father, mother and me all sat in the living room of our farmhouse. I was at our living room table reading a book. Mother sat across the table from me, knitting. Father sat at his usual spot at the table between mother and me. I remember being some worried that mother would tell father about me visiting the gypsies earlier that day and that I would be in a special kind of trouble with father again.

That didn't happen.

If mother had planned to spill the beans to father she just didn't get to it before the weather outside took a change for the worse. A storm rolled in and soon we were hearing loud booms of thunder and watching bright lightening flashes add the occasional look of daylight to the inside of our home.

I remember the conversation that night. Father said he had never counted on such trouble when he moved us from Connecticut to southeast Kansas some several years earlier. As she had done many times before, mother implored father to move us elsewhere, saying such a hostile country was no place to raise a boy. Father replied that he was done with pulling up stakes.

Of a sudden, as we watched strange shadows dance across our lantern-lit walls, we heard the thundering hooves of riders approach the house. We heard the sound even above the cracking thunder.

Then we heard a loud voice demand father come outside.

Father rose from his chair, stepped to the front door, opened it and then walked out onto the front porch. I stood behind him in the doorway.

Six riders sat their horses as thunder, lightning and rain filled the air. It was the Campseys and the Ferbers — the Regulators — their faces occasionally visible amidst the lightning flashes.

"Hello, Eaton! This is Shannon Campsey. Regulators."

"I know who you are. You and your men gave me this limp."

"Then limp out where we can see you, you stinkin' bastard. There's somethin' we need to tell you."

Father then walked to the edge of the porch.

"Well now, damn you! You got this comin'! When are you flat-headed blue-bellies gonna learn you don't tangle with Regulators, huh?"

Of a sudden, them sonsabitches commenced to firing at father and his body crumpled to the ground. They filled father full of bullet holes, shot him down like a durn mad dog. I ran over to father and fell on top of him, crying my eyes out and screaming. About that time, Wyley Campsey dismounted and came over and pulled me from atop father. Then he gave me a good whipping with his bullwhip. Shannon called Wyley off me or else he would've killed me for sure. Once Wyley had coiled up his whip, he pulled both sidearms and emptied all of his remaining rounds into father's body. Before they all rode off, Wyley looked directly into my eyes and said, "Your day is comin', and it's comin' damn soon."

Mother had already left the doorway of

the house. As them murdering skunks rode off, mother fell on top of father and screamed and cried her eyes out. She tried yelling something to those cowardly sonsabitches as they rode away but she couldn't get the words out, so overcome as she was by shock and terror.

I was eight years old, just a kid of a boy, when I saw father gunned down like a cur. I gotta tell you something. I'm an old man and there has never been a day that I haven't recalled that grisly scene from so many years ago. It's a thing what stays with a man and haunts him always.

I also carried nightmares from that night for many years after that awful night, horrible pictures constantly reminding me of that dreadful night so many years ago when I was a kid of a boy. I see those bastard snakes to this day. I see the four Campseys and the two Ferbers over and over again. They've never left me. These dreams forever remind me of their grisly smiles, their evil laughs. I even relive the storm. I hear once again father telling mother that he is too old to pull up stakes again and that this is his last stand. The thunder shakes the earth and the lightning flashes light up the inside of our farmhouse. Strange shadows dance along our living room walls and these shadows blend with the flickering of light from the candles and lanterns and lightning. The thundering hooves from outside repeat again and again, and the sound gets louder as its nears the farmhouse. When the riders reach the farmhouse, I hear them as if they are here at this very moment.

Amongst all that, devil and death tarot cards dance along the walls with the strange shadows and the flickering light. And I hear the words, the awful words spoken that night.

I hear Shannon Campsey tell father, "Well now, damn you! You got this comin'! When are you flat-headed blue-bellies gonna learn you don't tangle with Regulators, huh?"

I hear all of it, over and over.

And, on top of all that I see and hear Wyley Campsey as he looks me in the eye and says, "Your day is comin', and it's comin' damn soon."

The inside of our living room becomes smoky and hazy.

The thunder and lightning is always there, the rain pours down like nothing you ever saw. It's like the rain Noah must've seen before he had to build that ark them bible men talk about. The Regulators sit atop their mounts as the bullet-riddled body of father lays on the ground beneath them. I look up into the eyes of Wyley Campsey and I hear the cracks of his bullwhip against the sound of the thunder and falling rain. I hear mother as her screams and cries tell of a woman who has lost everything.

In a strange kind of way, these nightmares were a lot worse when I was a kid of a boy. You ever have a dream at night and you know full well it's a dream? That's how it got to be with me and these nightmares. The nightmare would come on like always and, as horrible as it was, I knew I was dreaming again. I would try to wake up and couldn't do it. The nightmare just kept going. As much as I would try to wake up and rise it felt as if something was holding me down strongly against my will and forcing me to live it once again. I saw the images and heard the sounds of the nightmare but knew I was lying on my back in bed and I couldn't move. I was trapped and it felt like a ton of bricks lay on top of me.

These night haunts terrified me for years and, truth be told, I ain't totally comfortable with them now. Leastways, the terror of it all eased a little as the years went slowly by.

Of course, of a day, when the sun cast its rays of light down to earth, I thought of them Regulators in a different way. I wasn't so deathly afraid of the thought of them. It was like my mind behaved one way during the darkness, and another way altogether during the light. I would see their evil grins and hear their hellish voices and a special kind of hatred boiled up within me. I loathed them bastard snakes!

A few days after father's murder, we buried his body in the ground of southeast Kansas.

The day of father's funeral proved to be a day that would define my future life.

Father had a friend named Mose Beaman, leader of the Vigilantes, who had stood by him through thick and thin. Mose had been to our place many times to help father as needs must over the years. Mose helped father with the farm work and Vigilante duties. He had often sat at our table and was practically a member of the family.

After the pastor had said his piece and after the last bit of dirt had been dropped down on father's box, Mose walked over to me and pulled me out of earshot of the others attending. There was fire in eyes that day the likes of which I had never seen before.

"Your father was a hard worker, Frank. You and I have it to do keeping this place up."

I told him I was a kid of a boy but also strong and able to pull my weight.

"Son, maybe together we can do the work of your father."

Mose extended his hand to mine and we shook on it.

"Frank, I have a question. Did you for sure get a look at the men who gunned down your father?"

"I saw their faces in the light of the lightning flashes. It was the four Campseys — Shannon, Jim, Jonce and Wyley. Them and the two Ferbers — Doc and John. I hate them."

"Did you say Wyley?"

"Yes, sir. He was there. Took a whip to me."

"That Wyley is poison mean, son. Shannon may be the leader, but that Wyley is a special kind of rattler. There's something I want to talk to you about."

"What is it?"

About that time, old Mose stares off in the distance. I could tell he had been contemplating something and hard-like.

"My boy, may an old man's curse rest upon you all the days of your life if you don't try to avenge the death of your father. You gotta kill them stinkin' sonsabitches."

"I will, Mr. Beaman. I promise, I will. I've

been thinking about that. Just as soon as I'm big enough and learn more about guns and shooting."

"That's where I come in. Here's your first gun, a cap and ball Navy revolver."

Mose opened a cloth sack and from within it pulled out the sidearm and handed it to me.

"I brought the Navy gun, son because it is lighter than the Army and the barrel is a little shorter. I think it will be better for you."

The Navy barrel ran about eight inches long while the Army barrel ran to about nine. Those Army and Navy guns were six-shooters. Old Mose fired the weapon and held it for me to see.

"Now, after the shot is fired and the gun is cocked," he said, "the chamber revolves and brings a new load under the hammer. That is why they are called revolvers."

Before the revolver, there was the pepper-box gun that had a revolving barrel. When the revolver came in the pepper-box gun went out. These days, those weapons seem primitive but, at the time, there were no better guns. It was just a matter of knowing how to use them effectively. At one time, the Indian held supremacy over man and beast with bows and flint-tipped arrows.

The bow and arrow wasn't much compared to the atom bomb, but at one time it was the best weapon around and those Indians knew how to use it!

"I'm gonna teach you how to shoot, mold bullets and eventually work this weapon without even looking down the sights."

"Mr. Beaman, this is fine!"

"Practice non-stop, here? When I see a lot of improvement I'll give you its mate and you can learn 'em both."

I ran my hands over that sidearm and got comfortable with the feel of it. From that point on, I worked that gun every chance I had. Me and Mose spent time practicing out in the woods and pastures. Mose set up the targets and I learned over time to hit my mark.

A few days after Mose gave me my first gun, he came by to teach me how to mold bullets. I was very happy to see him and was interested to see what he had brought. He set out a can of gunpowder, three boxes of caps, a lot of lead, a pair of bullet molds and a melting ladle. We set all of that on a bench beside the house and commenced to building a fire.

Mose put lead into the ladle and put it over the fire to melt. When the lead got hot, he poured it into the bullet mold and let it set for a few seconds. Then, he dropped out the finished, molded bullet. As soon as he had finished one, he closed the mold and poured it full of lead again. The bullets came out beautiful — and hot! We had to wait a bit before we could handle them. Then, we cut the neck off and the bullet was ready to use. Mose taught me to save the neck lead to use for additional bullets.

We kept the gunpowder in a powder horn to keep it dry. The horn was fastened to a strap that hung over the shoulder. At the small end of the horn was a removable cover that we called a charger. The charger was a measure that, when full, showed you just how much powder to use to fire the bullet.

You pour the powder into the chamber of the revolver, put in the molded bullet and ram it down with your ramrod, then put the cap on and you are ready to go. I learnt how to do all of this and Mose was some approving of my work.

Of course, I got to work learning that gun. Close to where we lived, there were these limestone ledges full of rattlesnakes. I soon boasted a box full of rattles from the snakes I had shot.

Mose came to visit one day and I showed him my box full of rattles and demonstrated how I could shoot off a snake's head with either hand.

True to his promise, he handed me the second gun, belt and holster complete. Took some time and a lot of practice, but it weren't no time until I was handling both weapons fairly comfortable-like. But, I never thought I had reached any kind of perfection with those sidearms. Mose made sure of that. Even a year after father's death, Mose was still around the farm a lot helping me with the work, so we practiced shooting every chance we got in between chores.

I always said that times were very hard for the snakes thereabouts, but we never killed game unless food was needed. All the guns were cleaned and loaded every night at our place, just as Mose had taught me.

And, that's how it was for many a year afterward. I tended to those sidearms while the other boys I knew thereabouts was tending to schoolwork. Over the many years to come, them pistols became extensions of my arms as I lived with the sole purpose of evening me a score.

5

By the time I was ready to set out on the trail for them Regulators some years later, mother had remarried and moved down to the Cherokee Nation of the Indian Territory.

That suited me just fine because I had heard a passel of them Regulators had moved down in the Nations, and with mother and my stepfather relocating there I would be right where I wanted to be. Turned out, the law had gotten a little too hot to handle up in Kansas for the Regulators and the likely answer for them was to relocate down to what is now Oklahoma to evade any real law and order.

Indian Territory, the country you and me are sitting in right now, stood as one of the most violent, one of the most lawless regions in the history of our country. I'm telling you boy, it was a hellhole. Fact, it was probably the worst, even compared to that country out near Tombstone in Arizona. At the time, this country was the last and wildest region on the North American continent.

Sure, them Cherokee, Choctaw, Creek, Chickasaw and Seminole Indians brought their tribal law to the territory when they were relocated here by the federal government many years ago, but the Indian courts held no sway with white men, and it was white men what were the biggest problem. The white men in the territory fell under the laws of the United States, and the United States government had no presence in the region until president Grant sent in Judge Isaac Parker to begin cleaning up the place.

So, up until then, the territory attracted every damned kind of outlaw mankind had ever known. If you were a non-Indian who came into this country back then, you were probably either a murderer, a gut robber, a whiskey peddler, a prostitute, or a rapist. Maybe even a combination of more than one.

So, it made sense that those Regulators decided to leave Kansas, where there was a system of law and order, and perambulate on down here into the Indian Territory. No one in the territory would hold them accountable for the crimes they committed in

Kansas or anywhere else, and bandits around the country knew it.

The day we left for the Indian Nations a helluva thing happened. Nine years had passed since father's murder and I reckon I was about seventeen years old. Mother, my stepfather, several helpers and me were loading up a couple of wagons near the farmhouse. Of a sudden, I took a look down to the trail and, lo and behold, there were those same colorful gypsy vardos ambling along just as they did nearly nine years before. I ran down to the trail and hailed the little caravans to a stop. Adelita was sitting atop the lead vardo with her grandfather.

Adelita had grown even more beautiful since last I had seen her. Her night-black hair damned near hugged the ground and her dark eyes were just as haunting as before, speaking of untold secrets and mysteries. Around her neck she wore that same colorful scarf she had used to hold her tarot cards that day so long ago, a scarf trimmed in colors of turquoise and red with pretty purple flowers against an orange background. It was a beautiful scarf, a work of art I wasn't likely to forget. I see it now just as vividly as I saw it then.

Adelita's grandmother emerged from the

back door of the lead vardo and I'll be damned if she didn't make the sign of the cross once she saw me. The sight of me must've scared the living hell out of that woman. She walked up and gave me an almost unhappy, appraising kind of look. I got the feeling she didn't like me too much, but she tried to be polite.

"My boy, you are older and have grown into a handsome Gitano. Adelita, look at this boy now — a boy who seems no longer a boy. You are not the farmer boy I remember."

I made a slight bow to the grandmother, greeted Adelita and turned back again to face the grandmother.

"I ain't going to be no farmer."

"I see that. Yet, there is something else different about you."

About that time, Adelita rose to a standing position atop the vardo and took a look up the hill to our farmhouse.

"I see wagons being loaded at your home."

"Yep, we're hitting the trail for the Cherokee Nation down south of here in the Indian Territory. Mother has wished to move there ever since the night father was killed and now she is married to a man what owns land down there and so off we go."

Adelita made notice of the sidearms hanging from my gun belt and then she clutched the rosary hanging around her neck under the colorful scarf.

"You now wear the huge pistolas. Why?"

"I've spent these many years learning them so I can track down and kill the men who murdered my father."

"When did this happen?"

"The night of that very day I met you and you read me the cards."

Right about then, Adelita's grandmother gave her a grave look and motioned her to sit back down atop the vardo.

"We must move on, child. Adelita, let us be on our way."

Turns out, Adelita had not only grown taller and prettier since I had last seen her, but she had also earned more esteem in her family and could speak up with her opinions when needs must.

"Wait, grandmother. We were to camp near here for a few nights, anyway. Can we not make camp here?"

Adelita's grandmother showed a look of resignation, turned around and walked away. I could sure tell she was some perturbed.

But, sure enough, them gypsy folks made camp right off that very spot that night and I was sure happy they did. Gave me time to visit with Adelita. I'm telling you, I just couldn't believe my good fortune of seeing her after all of those long, hard years. Just as she was to me on that first meeting long before, she was to me again — a bright, shiny, mysterious and beautiful spot in a dull, gloomy, hardened world.

I spent that evening with Adelita, and that is a night I will never forget. Adelita's grandmother, along with the other women of the family, cooked up several Dutch ovens full of rabbit goulash and we enjoyed the feast. They ate the bread, passed the wine and danced the night away with pure joy. The men of the camp were master guitar and fiddle players, and Adelita's grandfather played a little flute, so the night air was filled with some of the happiest music I had ever heard in my life.

In a strange kind of way, though, the music was a mix of pure joy mixed with a tinge of sorrow. That fiddle playing would go along up-tempo-like and folks would dance with joy, but right in the midst of the fast beat the fiddle would draw down a little mournful lick before taking off hell for leather again. The music gave one to know that this life has its happy moments, but that it's right in the middle of those fine times — the sweet moments of life we remember when we are old — that the sad times come without any notice. And, maybe that gypsy music was saying that we should brush off them gloomy periods, muy pronto, and get back to dancing life's dance again.

Those were my thoughts as I enjoyed the music and had myself one hell of a time tapping my toes to the gypsy rhythm.

Adelita saw me enjoying myself and told me I would make a good gypsy and how come did I not join them on their journeys across the plains and mountains?

Before I could answer, she grabbed me up and drug me out to the area around the campfire to dance. I tried holding back out of shyness but she yanked me out there anyway. She said she wanted to teach me the Flamenco dance, so I resigned myself that I was going to learn the Flamenco dance before the sun came up the next day. Once out there in front of all of her family, we commenced to dancing as a couple, her leading and me following.

While out there clumsily trying to do what Adelita told me, I looked over ringside and saw Stevo, Adelita's cousin, staring at me in a none-too-happy manner, like maybe I was infringing on his hunting grounds. Adelita seemed to pay him no nevermind, so I decided I would do the same. I figured she knew the situation better than me.

My first round of dancing was an embarrassment, so I was naturally more than ready to go sit down for a spell when Adelita wanted to rest. We sat down with our backs against one of the vardo wheels and drank from the flask.

She pulled out her tarot cards, the same deck she had used on our first meeting roughly nine years before, and read me more fortunes. Then she pulled out a regular deck of playing cards and charmed me to no end with her card tricks and slight-of-hand trickery. She had been taught well by her family. She told me there had been many times her family had relied on card tricks and such to make money. I believed her. She was a deft card sharp.

After a bit, Adelita pulled me back out to the campfire to dance. This time, I was some better. I had learned the moves and was keeping up with Adelita step for step and move for move. While we swirled and stepped, moving this way and that, I couldn't help but notice Stevo leaving the scene in disapproval, returning to within one of the vardos. That didn't stop us none. We kept it up long into the night, dancing and talking under the canopy of a starlit sky.

There came a time when the campfire dulled and the fiddle and guitar players turned in for the night. Not wanting to wake anyone, we spoke in low whispers.

Adelita commenced telling me all about her people, all about where they had come from originally, all about their language, and all about their experiences with folks down through the years. She told me how much she enjoyed the traveling life of a gypsy. She and her folks held no notions about planting roots in any one place. She said that many people they had encountered had some difficulty in reconciling with this kind of life and often held it against her and her folks.

She told me her people came to Mexico many years ago from Spain. Before Spain, her ancestors had been in India, she said.

Adelita's people spoke pretty good English, but they often took off talking in a language that was a mix of recognizable Spanish words and words from their other ancestors from Europe. I couldn't make heads or tails of it most of the time, although I would occasionally pick up on a Spanish word I had heard before. Today, folks call their particular language Spanish-Romani, but I didn't hear people call it that back then. I just figured it was their special language and I accepted it as such.

In the time I knew Adelita, I picked up on a few of their words. There was churumbel for baby, chaval for boy, garito for gambling den, galochi for heart, and jalar meaning "to eat." That is just some of the words I picked up from her. Of course, I also learned a few of them gypsy curse words, but I won't repeat any of that here. Adelita's brothers were skilled in the use of those.

You know, those gypsy folk often used their language as a sort of secret code language amongst themselves when they didn't want bystanders to understand what they were saying. Adelita scolded her folks a few times for taking off in that language while I was around that night. She told them it was rude to do that when I was company. To be honest, though, it didn't bother me at all. I figured it was a people's right to speak in whatever language they were capable.

Fact, I enjoyed hearing Adelita speaking in that language with her beautiful, singsong voice. When she spoke those puzzling words with her mysterious voice it gave me to know that I was in the company of a special kind of woman, a sort of raven-haired, dark-eyed princess from a far away land. In a land of farmers, ranchers, cowboys and outlaws, Adelita stood out to me as a mystifying sort, what with her dark hair and eyes, olive skin, tarot cards, flamenco music, and wandering life on the trail.

Adelita believed her people came from those who possessed an ancient magical knowledge and kept the old magical secrets, and that this awareness passed down through certain ones of her people and that she herself carried this understanding in her mind and heart and soul. It was the power of her ancestors living within her.

She said she could not only tell a fortune but also cast a spell, or what she called an amria, when needs must. She said a gypsy spell is a hard one to lick. I didn't have no reason to doubt her. To boot, I figured to stay on her good side and not give her any reason to cast a spell on me, as life was hard enough as it was.

Leastways, I was some smitten with her and her enchanting ways, and I don't know too many fellows who would not have been.

Adelita told me her ancestors left Spain for Argentina many years before and eventually made their way to Mexico and then up the famous El Camino Real de Tierra Adentro to the United States. She told me her people had a long history of never being understood and accepted by folks and that they had been driven out of different places down through the years.

They'd been driven out of places in Europe way back when, they'd been sent packing down in Mexico a time or two, and they'd been forced to make dust many times in the United States by people who accused them of stealing, cheating folks in business deals, and sorcery.

She told me they had been told to skedaddle out of many a frontier town for sometimes the flimsiest of reasons. I wasn't too happy to hear that my sweet Adelita and her people had been made to endure such hardships. When she told me these stories it made me want to be with her always so that I could protect her. It also made me think of my own parents who frowned on mingling with gypsy folks. That fact gave me to know that such harsh notions about gypsies was a strong thing on our frontier in those days and even now in these times.

One thing I figured out about Adelita's people early on was that they practiced their old magical ways right along with some of the ways of the Christian church. I had seen Adelita's grandmother make the sign of the cross more than once and I had heard her utter special Catholic prayers of protection and such. She and Adelita carried their rosaries with them at all times and I knew they prayed the rosary often. I didn't know what to think about all of that back then, but I later met Indian folks out in New Mexico and Arizona who also practiced a sort of combination of their ancient Indian mysticism along with practices of the Catholic Church.

She and I sat under the night sky and talked long into the night. I learned a whole lot about her and her folks, their way of life, how they looked at things, and I sort of compared it to the life I had lived up until then. I began to figure there was something to be said for their way. Father and mother had worked hard all their lives to make a place for themselves in this world and what had it gotten them? It had gotten them a life full of toil and hardship and it put father into an early grave. I was some starting to see the advantages of living a life of traveling around and seeing the sights.

And the thought of doing that with the likes of a beautiful and mysterious girl like Adelita made a certain kind of sense.

Of course, I told Adelita all about father's murder and how I planned to start evening the score, muy pronto.

"Once mother gets settled down in the Nations, that's when I hit the trail for them."

"Even if you kill each of them, your father is still gone and you cannot bring him back. Come with me instead and live the life of a gypsy. You were made to be one of us."

Now, I gotta tell you, that idea was some pleasing to me. I couldn't think of any other life I wanted to live right there at that moment, and I was sure pondering over joining up with Adelita and her folks right then. But, I had lived for too many years with a single purpose in mind, and that was to hunt down each of the men who had murdered father and even the score. I had never really contemplated what life would hold for me after I took care of that business, I just knew I had a job to do and that was that.

"I'll join with you as soon as I've done the job. I'll make quick work of it so I can get back with you muy pronto."

"We travel to many places, sometimes with no rhyme or reason. How will you find me?"

"I will find you if I have to search the entire country."

"My grandfather often mentions Albuquerque. Mentions going there. Something about seeing the Royal Road, whatever that is. Plus, the cards tell me we will be there."

"It's settled then. Albuquerque is where I go if I can't find you anywhere else."

"There is something else I must tell you. It is my family's desire that I marry my cousin, Stevo. I am not certain my heart is tied with his, but time and family may settle the question for me. Such is the way with our people sometimes. I hope I see you again, Frank Eaton. I hope I see you soon."

"Trust those cards. I will find you."

When the sun arose the next day, it felt good to have a single, clear-cut mission in life. I stretched the kinks out, had my breakfast and coffee, and pondered how great the life is for a man whose main reason for living is hunting and killing Regulators.

6

We had been living in the Cherokee Nation of the Indian Territory for only a few months before I set out on the trail of my intended prey.

I left our place on Sand Creek in the Cooweescoowee District in the Cherokee Nation one fine morning with the intention of riding to Fort Gibson. There, I could hear news of the trail and possibly learn the exact location of those whose hides I planned to bore full of lead. To boot, just to make sure I was at the top of my game in the shooting department, I wanted to check my shooting skills against those of some of them soldier boys at the fort. I wanted to know for sure in my heart I was up for the job at hand. As determined as I was to even the score, I knew for sure that tracking this bunch of stink cat bastards was some serious business that could get my ass killed. I had already seen what they were capable of doing and the images of it haunted me then and now. I didn't plan on botching the job.

Them folks at Fort Gibson was responsible for keeping the peace in the country thereabouts, a job they had been doing since the fort was built back in 1824. Back then, the federal government gave Fort Gibson an area in which to keep the peace between the Osage and Cherokee Indians. Them Osages had been around that country for quite awhile, for maybe thousands of years, while them Cherokee folks was new thereabouts. There was never any trouble in that regard, so I figured them soldier boys and their commanders had done their job. Years later, the fort was reinforced to keep that part of the territory free from the murderers and marauders what had stormed into the country in the years following the War Between the States. The men at the fort kept their eyes and ears on everything going on in that country, and I figured they might just know where I could find myself some Regulators. It only made sense that I make my first stop there.

I rode up to the fort and took in all the sights and sounds of a frontier fort of that day. There were cavalry stables, barracks, officers' quarters, a powder magazine, a chapel, a hospital and a guardhouse.

I checked in at the guardhouse and one of the guards asked me my business.

"May I see the fort's commander?"

"That'd be Colonel Copinger. Why do you need him?"

"I'm in the information business — delivering and collecting."

"What's your name?"

"The name is Frank Eaton."

"Heard of you. You from Kansas?"

"Formerly. My family now lives near Sand Creek, Cooweescoowee District right here in the Cherokee Nation."

"Heard what happened to your father many years ago. Did his murderers ever swing for what they done?"

"No, but I believe some of them are down here in the Indian Territory these days, or at least that's what I've heard. But that is why I'm here."

"Come on in. I'll take you to Colonel Copinger."

The guard walked me inside the fort and along a boardwalk to the Colonel's office. Copinger was standing outside in front of his office when we got there. He was a distinguished looking gentleman in his military get-up — tall, well-groomed gray hair and mustache. Standing beside him was a tall, law-and-order-looking man whose coat lapel bore a lawman's badge placed above a shiny piece of Masonic jewelry.

"Sir, this gentleman is Frank Eaton. He wishes to speak with you."

About that time, Copinger took a few silent moments to meditate on the words he had just heard, like he was trying to go back and snag something from memory.

"Should I know you?"

"Good to meet you, colonel. You might've heard of my late father, Francis Eaton. Folks called him Frank. He was murdered some years ago up in Kansas."

"That's it. Murdered by men calling themselves some kind of so-called Confederate sympathizers."

"They called themselves Regulators. Still do, I hear."

"A sad day, to be sure. But welcome to Indian Territory. What brings you here?"

"We don't live in Kansas anymore. My family lives near Sand Creek in the Cooweescoowee District not far from here. I'm wanting to make sure I'm brushed up on a few things, maybe obtain some information."

"Does this have to do with your father?"

"It does."

"I don't like the sound of what your plans might be in this. What kind of information do you seek?"

"I'll come right out with it, colonel. I made a vow to hunt down each of the men who shot down father and settle the score . . ."

"Hold on there, boy. Do I hear you right that you intend to gun those men down in revenge?"

"No sir. You hear me right that I intend to gun down these men to fulfill a vow I made to settle a score. They'll get more than a fair fight, and that's a lot more than they gave father who they shot down like a durn mad dog."

"What information do you seek, then?"

"Their whereabouts. I hear some of those six men are down here in the Indian Nations. I hear one is over in Missouri tending bar, and another — Wyley Campsey — well, I hear he is out in Albuquerque dealing faro or some such. I want to take care of the four closest to me and then make social calls on the two who vamoosed out of the country."

"These men — these Regulators — they murder for pleasure. And I've heard of Wyley Campsey. He makes the lot of them look like store clerks. I won't provide information for such an endeavor."

"But I will."

It was the voice of the rough looking lawman with the badge and the shiny Masonic jewelry on his lapel. Colonel Copinger spoke up.

"Forgive me. I haven't introduced you to Marshal Chris Adams, one of Judge Parker's men out of Fort Smith. He's a straight law and order man — I thought — as you should be, also."

That was the first time for me to stand in the company of one of Judge Parker's officers. I had heard all about them. They were tough men, working for a tough judge, hunting some of the most dangerous and vile men in the history of the great western frontier.

They called Parker the "Hanging Judge" for good reason. He was assigned by the president of the United States to head to Fort Smith and set up a court to deal with the droves of murderers, robbers, cattle rustlers, prostitutes, whiskey peddlers and rapists what roamed the Indian Territory in those days. Every kind of bandit from all across the country set up shop in Indian Territory because it was a land free of any "White Man's Court." Up until the time of Judge Parker, the only justice dealt out in Indian Territory was out of an Indian court for Indian lawbreakers.

That left easy pickings for any criminal

who was not an Indian. Sheer terror reigned supreme in these parts. It was a hell on earth.

Leastways, Judge Parker got to Fort Smith and commenced a house cleaning. He tried them, convicted them and hung them, muy pronto, in many cases. He hung as many as six men on his famous gallows at once. People traveled from all across the region to witness his hangings. There were crowds as large as five-thousand people what filled the streets of Fort Smith on hanging days.

The courthouse from which Parker dealt justice sits right there on a pretty little spot near Garrison Avenue where the Poteau meets the Arkansas River. The famous gallows are located on the courthouse grounds to this day.

Parker was responsible for administering justice in what was known as the Western Judicial District of Arkansas. That included counties in the westernmost sections of Arkansas, seventy-thousand square miles of Indian Territory, and a strip fifty-miles wide along the southern boundary of Kansas.

That was a lot of dirt to cover and it took a lot of hardened officers to make it happen. Many of them lost their lives trying to capture these wanton and desperate banditos and bring them back to Fort Smith for trial. Some of the marshals were war veterans, some were former cowboys and ranchers, but most all of them knew every crack and crevice of Indian Territory and were willing to face the risks of the job head on with often times very little pay. The business of Judge Parker's officers was damned tough and so I was some proud to finally meet one of the marshals in person.

I shook the lawman's hand and his was the firm handshake of one who took his job seriously right down to the ground — a no-nonsense fellow, but one who played strictly by the rules. I got the feeling right away that maybe he played more by the rules than I wanted to insofar as the Campseys and Ferbers were concerned. But, right away, he sounded like maybe he could help with my cause. The marshal extended his hand to mine and then asked me my business.

"You're looking for those Campseys and Ferbers?"

"I am. I know each and every one of their faces by heart."

"Maybe I can help you. I've heard of those names being right here in the Cherokee Nation. I've also heard about those Regulators, heard their numbers might've grown since relocating down here in the Nations. Wanna go in cahoots? I think I know where one or two of 'em hole up."

I'll be honest. I didn't know if I wanted to work as team going after them Regulators, but I needed someone to help me navigate this country since I was a relative newcomer to it. I just gave Marshal Adams a firm "maybe." That's when Colonel Copinger broke in.

"Son, you said you also came here to get brushed up on something. What do you mean?"

"I want to make sure I'm brushed up on my shooting before I set out on the trail. Figured I might learn some things from you and your men."

"Son, you'd better be first rate right now, going up against their like. It's too late to think about brushing up at this late date."

About that time, Marshal Adams broke back in and suggested they take a look at the shooting cards I was holding.

"Colonel, whataya say we have ourselves a little shooting contest outside the grounds here — you, me and Frank here? Let's see what he's got."

"Sure. We can always use the practice. But don't think this is my approval of the boy setting out for the Campseys and the Ferbers, though. Let's step outside the fort and start out with rifles."

So, the colonel started barking out orders to his men, telling them to step outside the fort and set up targets for rifle practice. A soldier soon showed up carrying a wood box full of tin cans. Him and a few others started setting up those cans at good rifle shooting distances.

The colonel yelled the order to set up about thirty cans. Once the soldiers had set up the targets, the colonel yelled out another order, this one a command for them to get the hell out of the way. Then, the colonel stepped over to me, handed me an 1873 Winchester and told me to go to work.

"You go first, Eaton. Hit the first six of those cans, starting from left to right."

I took the rifle, ran my fingers along the stock and barrel a few times, and held the weapon for a moment just to get the feel of it. Then, I examined the can targets and began firing from a standing position, working the lever as I went. I hit five of the six cans before handing the weapon back to the colonel.

"That's fair, son. But nothing exceptional. Marshal, you're next. Use the same rifle and hit the next six."

The colonel handed the rifle to Marshal Adams and the lawman commenced firing his way to a six out of six score. Marshal

Adams handed the rifle back to Copinger and the good colonel went about hitting six out of six, also.

"Son, you see how me and the Marshal massacred those cans one by one in short order? That's the kind of shooting required when going up against the likes of those who killed your father."

Well, I gotta tell you. I had been practicing with my sidearms nearly every day for almost nine years, but had only used rifles for hunting and such. I knew I was decent with rifles, as good as most if not a shade better when it came right down to it. But in all those years of practicing, in all those years of contemplating how I was going to face them Regulators down, I never imagined standing off at a distance and picking them off with a rifle. No sir. I said as much to Copinger.

"But I don't plan on using rifles, Colonel. I plan on using my pistols, up close, oily and slick-like. Throw a can out there a ways."

Copinger tossed a can about forty feet out in front of us and I went to work. Fanning that hammer, I hit that can twice on the ground before it went to flying in the air. Still fanning, I went about hitting that can four more times before it hit the ground. I re-holstered that pistol and pulled the one on my left.

"Colonel, toss one up in the air."

Let me tell you, ol' Copinger was some shocked and bewildered, but he tossed that can up there and I went to work again. It sounded like thunder going off as I hit and redirected that can five times as it jerked this way and that above us before hitting the ground. I hit that can one more time after it landed and them onlookers knew they had just seen some good shooting. Them soldier boys whooped it up while Copinger and Adams just stood there with their mouths ajar.

I overheard them soldiers as they discussed what they just saw.

"Son of a bitch! Who is that kid?"

"They say his name is Frank Eaton. He's hunting the men who gunned his pa down some years ago."

I walked over to Chris Adams and asked him what he thought.

"God Almighty, Frank! You know there's better weaponry available these days, don't you? You don't need to fool around with that cap and ball contraption no longer."

"I can't afford them Colt Peacemakers."

"Well, I got two brand new ones for you. Took 'em off a man I brought in to Fort

Smith for hangin'. They're in my saddle bags."

"Sounds like they didn't bring the man you brought in to Fort Smith any luck."

Adams laughed.

"Eaton, you're a damned sight better with sidearms than he was, I'll assure you."

"Alright, then. I'll accept those pistols. That makes us pards."

Adams gave me my new weapons and I knew I would have to practice with them to get the feel of the weight. They were superior pistols and, in time, would serve me and my cause a whole lot better, but I knew I needed practice to become as good with them as I was with the ones ol' Mose Beaman gave me. Adams then walked over to Copinger.

"Colonel, whataya think?"

"Damned good with the rifles, but masterful with the sidearms. Never seen anything like it. I'm giving you a new name, Frank. You're a damned Pistol Pete."

As I sit back and think about that these many years later, I guess it was kind of funny that I had earned a marksman's nickname of honor and had done nothing to earn it up to that point except bore holes into a box full of tin cans.

"Compliments appreciated, Colonel."

"Son, there's no denying you're some special with those pieces, but I want you to think about what you're doing when you talk about facin' down Regulators. Like Adams says, I've heard their numbers might've grown, too. And that Wyley Campsey — well just fight shy of him."

"I respect what you're saying. Believe me, I see Wyley's face every day, and there's a part of me that wants never to see him again."

"Then leave it be. You're plannin' your own funeral. That Wyley is a cold-blooded murderer — and lightning fast, to boot."

"No, sir, I have it to do. I'll finish the six who did for father or die in the trying."

Adams broke in to say we would work as a team as long as we agreed to take any Regulators we found in alive. I told Adams there weren't any way in hell the men who gunned down father would be taken in alive to anywhere. I could tell by the look in Adams' eyes and the sound of his words that he didn't believe me none at all.

"We do this the way Judge Parker likes, and that's the law and order way. We can work as a team, but I don't want the fact that these men murdered your father to tempt you to cross the line."

"I'll tell you what. If we find the men

we're both looking for, then we'll go in calling and they will come out dancing whatever jig they decide is best. But I'll wager whatever amount you like that they won't come willing."

"Fair enough. When are you wanting to start?"

"I've waited these many years and I don't want to tarry another day. Let's start tonight."

"I see you mean business and that's just fine with me."

Me and Adams shook hands with the good Colonel and bade him farewell. I never seen him again, but I'll never forget his words to Adams as the Marshal and I rode out of the fort.

"Adams, be careful he doesn't do more than assist you, or else you'll be assisting him."

7

Adams and I made camp that night on the banks of the Arkansas River amidst a cropping of cottonwood and willows grown up out of a carpet of Indian grass. Me, I started working those new sidearms of mine, testing the play and feel of the hammer, trigger and cylinder of each, gauging the balance of the weapon with both hands. I sure liked the way they felt, and knew that, with practice, I would be better gunned for the job at hand than with my old weapons. The thought made me feel good. It gave me added confidence as I contemplated facing down those Campseys and Ferbers. Those gnarly, stinking sonsabitches!

That's something I had done many times over during the years since father's death. I thought of each of his murderers and what I would do and say as I faced them for the first time as a man ready to settle the score. Consequences be damned. Over and over throughout my young years the scenes played out in my mind with me working those pistols to as much perfection as possible. Every word and move was etched not only to memory but within my very existence. I thought about it during the day and in my thoughts and dreams at night. Even at the dinner table and while sitting in church.

You ever met someone with a goal or dream that eats at them every second of every day? Maybe it's a kid you grow up with who wants to go to college. Maybe it's that fellow who wants to be a famous singer. Maybe it's someone who wants to grow up and be like one of them astronaut fellows we hear the news people talk about. Some of them make their dreams come true and others don't. Those that make it are those who get up every day and tell themselves that they will succeed and that's just the way it is, and then they go about making it happen with study and practice. They think about it morning, noon and night. And if they truly want it to happen then it surely will.

That was me. I lived with one idea in mind and one only, and that was to ventilate me some Campseys and Ferbers! I knew what I wanted to say to each of them and I knew how I wanted to make my first move when the time came. And there I was out in the middle of the Cherokee Nation of the Indian Territory with Marshal Chris Adams and we were about to go hunt some Regulators! That was the kind of business meant for a young fellow named Frank Eaton and I was sure ready to get started.

Adams said that some of them Regulators was right there in the Cherokee Nation not too far from where we were at. Man, when he told me that I started getting butterflies in my belly, kind of like them football players get right before the first game of the season, or like them boxers right before they step into the ring for the big fight against a real bruiser. That described me right then. I wanted to get going in the worst way, but I had them butterflies fluttering this way and that inside me!

Adams watched me working them new pistolas and was some interested in the sight that fine evening.

"In a few days, you're gonna be right good with them Colts."

"Gonna take some getting use to."

"Just stay at it. Any man who handles antiques like you will deal hell with those Peacemakers in no time."

"Seems like my whole life has been spent

learning pistols."

"Don't know that I have you figured, Frank. You say you want to even the score with these men but I just don't take you as the vicious kind. I don't see the hate in your eyes at all."

"I quit hating them a long time ago. Man can't live with hate like that."

"Interesting. But you've been preparing for this for a long time."

"Night and day for years. I've got it to do. Made a promise to an old man and to myself to get it evened up."

"An old man? Who'd that be?"

"Mose Beaman, father's best friend. Mose said an old man's curse was on me all the days of my life if I didn't settle it or die trying."

"Did this Mose say anything about Wyley Campsey?"

"He's the worst of the lot, I know."

Night fell on the Indian Territory, and we were only able to see the river because of the moonlight on the water when our eyes were away from the fire. The drone of red-eyed cicadas filled the night with only the occasional hoot of a nearby owl. It sounded like that owl was asking, "Who cooks for you? Who cooks for you?"

"Frank, whataya say we bring 'em all in

alive? Take 'em over to Fort Smith and let Judge Parker hang 'em?"

"Not likely, I'm thinking."

"Seems like I remember that some of the men you're after are wanted by the Cherokee Nation for cattle rustling and such."

"The men who gunned down father like a mongrel dog will not be taken anywhere alive."

"Leastways, we can try. Judge Parker wants law and order brought to the Indian Territory. He sees an end to the days of the lawless gun. And I agree with him."

"Okay. We'll call the play. Ask them to come peaceable. They'll come out dancing as needs must."

"The two closest to us right now are Shannon Campsey and Doc Ferber. They're holed up north of here. Not even a day's ride. You game?"

"I've got it to do. Let's start the play tomorrow."

"Alright, first things first. Hold up your right hand."

"What?"

"We gotta swear you in as a Deputy United States Marshal. You're about to be on the payroll of Judge Isaac Parker, United States District Judge responsible for ridding the Indian Territory of horse thieves, whiskey peddlers and murderers."

Adams had information that, by early afternoon of the following day, had led us to the ramshackle cabin of none other than Shannon Campsey.

It was about then that I realized that I was scared to no end. I had lived all those years thinking about running these men down and tying off what needed tying. I had worked with those pistols for so long that my hands felt empty without them. Now, here I was wondering what in the hell had I gotten myself into. I thought about Adelita, and asked myself why had I left her for such a job as this, a job that could end up with me owning a permanent place in the Indian Territory, a nice cool place six feet underground and with a belly full of lead. The fear took a sort of back seat as Adams and I took stock of the job at hand.

From behind our perch of brush, brambles, rocks and small trees, roughly fifty yards out from the front cabin door, we could smell beef cooking and see smoke bellowing from the smokestack. We sat there for about an hour appraising the situation when, of a sudden, a fellow walked out from inside the cabin onto the front porch. It was Shannon Campsey just as sure as I'm sitting here, and he looked about how I thought he would look those many years later.

He was still sporting that fancy mustache of his with the swirled ends and had something of a goatee. He appeared even rougher looking and more unkempt since that night I last saw him. Even from my spot behind the brush and rocks fifty yards away I could see he still wore those fancy boots with the shafts decorated with the tarot cards, and he kept his trousers tucked in them so he could be identified with the rest of his Regulator friends, I reckon. Those fancy boots showing off them tarot cards seemed to be one of their calling cards.

He looked this way and that real careful-like, inspecting the line of trees on either side of the cabin as well as the area of brush, trees and rocks where Adams and I lay hidden. I was some tempted to ventilate him right there where he stood, but the thought vanished like a puff of smoke as soon as the murdering bastard stepped back inside the cabin.

I had a bad feeling about the set up that day and told Adams so. He just sort of ignored me and asked if I was ready.

"Ready? Ready for what?"

"Let's walk up and introduce ourselves. They don't know who we are or who we're after. Let's get in close and take whoever is in there without too much of a fight."

"I don't want to get bore full of holes while we're walking up to the front porch."

"I'm just followin' protocol."

"I don't like your protocol none at all. I'll bet Shannon has guards out and about in these trees watching the place. Walking straight up to the front door is like asking to be ventilated. Let's don't be so damned direct. I mean, if there are sentries in these woods we're liable to get riddled with lead anyway, but I don't want to be out there in the open walking up to the front door."

"Okay, you go left and I'll go right. We circle around to the other end of the cabin and powwow after we get a better look at the layout."

So, we both begin slowly walking out from each side of our position. Sweat poured down my face as I took first one step and then two. Sure as hell, from the woods on my side a flurry of gunfire comes pouring in. One of the rounds creased Adams' leg and he fell to the ground. Had we ambled out of the cover of our rocks and brush to approach the front door those guards would have blown him to the hereafter. I was fairly glad we kept to at least some cover the way we did.

Adams wasn't so far away that I couldn't reach him pretty quick. I ran over there, lifted him up and carried him back to our original position behind the brush and rocks and small trees with lead whistling all around. Once I set him down, I took a closer look at the layout. Right quick-like, I saw that if I backed up about thirty feet from our perch and then swung around and to the back of the left side of those trees I would be out of sight of those gunmen. I could outflank them. That's what I determined to do. But, this time, I intended to go slow and low to the ground, crawling-like.

I took out at a slow crawl, keeping it quiet. I made my way through the rocks and brush, weaving this way and that, and stopping every now and again to take stock of what lay around me. My eyes scoured every inch of the layout on all sides and my ears were open for the slightest sounds. The sweat poured down from my face because I was some concerned with the situation we had walked right into. Using my elbows as best I could to move me forward, I started out again. About that time, the weight of my body snapped a twig into and, to me, it sounded like a cannon firing. I came to a sudden stop, my eyes as big as silver dollars and sweat dripping from my face like a waterfall.

I crawled further along, trying to make no sound at all in doing so. It was slow going but I didn't mind that. I figured I had all day to get this right. From behind me came a sound of something stirring in the leaves. I froze right there on the spot, afraid to even pivot my head around to see what it was. I finally turned around enough to spy the area from which the sound came. All I could see was an ancient cottonwood and nothing at all moving around it. I heard the sound again and knew that it came from behind that huge tree. I'm telling you for true, the sweat dripped off my face and my heart pounded like a war drum, and the pounding of the beats in my ears was unsettling.

I brought both pistols to bear and stayed down on my belly waiting for the target to show itself. I remained there for the longest time before a squirrel darted from behind the tree and went along its merry way. I relaxed a bit upon seeing that squirrel, but not for long. I had to keep moving to get myself in behind where that gunfire came from. So off I went again, slowly, quietly.

Soon, I was comfortable in knowing I had reached that spot. I had crawled right up to a tree trunk and remained there for a while, listening and watching. I finally determined that the view was no good from my lying down position and that, like it or not, I was just going to have to stand up. I had gotten kind of comfortable down there in my safe spot on the ground.

I made all the safe, slow movements to get myself off the ground and into a standing position against that tree, and that exercise alone seemed to last an eternity with me being careful not to make a sound.

Once to my feet, I began navigating around trees and boulders until I finally came up behind our ambushers. With their rifles aimed and at the ready, and with their backs to me, three gunmen lay there facing our original position in front of the cabin. They must have thought they saw Adams moving and making a target because they all three commenced to firing a steady stream of rounds his direction.

I figured it was time to announce myself, and I remembered those words of Shannon Campsey from that day long ago when they robbed that bank and shot father in the leg.

"Swing your partners, boys! Ladies to the center!"

All to once, these bushwhackers began turning around to face me and that's when I shot them to a man, two through the chest and the slow one who couldn't get turned around fast enough right in the back. Served the son of a bitch right, I thought, for firing on us ambush-like. Once I had inspected all the bodies, and was certain they were down for good, I retraced my route back to Adams who was still exactly where I left him. He had moved around a little and that told me he wasn't seriously wounded. Just creased. Right off, he wanted to know how I eliminated those ambushers.

"Took me forever, but I made my way to the rear of the three gunmen laying crouched and ready for us. They'd been watching for us for the longest time as we ambled in here."

"And, then?"

"They began firing in your direction and I ended it."

"You shot them in the back?"

"The two who turned around to face me took it in the chest, the other one in the back. I wasn't making much of a distinction at the time."

"We don't shoot men in the back."

Well, I have to tell you, I was some perplexed that Adams would say something like that. Those men were firing on his position and I determined to stop it, and muy pronto. To boot, those bastards were turning around to fire at me and they meant business. At the time, I figured Adams worked just a shade too much by the book, and passed his remark off without letting it bother me. I was also wondering if I was smart to have gone in cahoots with him. I didn't need any hindrances, and I certainly didn't need him criticizing my every move. I had a score to settle and didn't care too much about the pleasantries. Anyhow, I just changed the subject.

"Okay, there's Shannon inside the cabin. I need to settle with him."

By that time, Adams had managed to get to his feet and was walking around without too much trouble. He called out to the cabin.

"Shannon Campsey! You still in there? Federal Marshal here outa Fort Smith."

We got nothing but a long period of silence and then Adams called out again.

"Campsey, we know someone is in there mindin' the fire! C'mon out!"

Again, we got nothing but the quiet of a peaceful afternoon. Total silence.

"Adams, betcha I can get him out. Watch this."

I cupped my hands around my mouth and let out a big yell toward the cabin.

"Shannon Campsey! My name is Frank

Eaton! I'll bet you remember me!"

Sure as hell, we heard the sound of a door opening and then footsteps on the cabin porch. From our perch behind the brush and rocks, we saw Shannon standing there on the porch with hands resting on his sidearms.

"Shannon, this is Frank Eaton! I'm coming on up."

I began walking on up and Adams chimed in.

"Eaton, what in hell are you doing?"

"I've messed around here long enough today. It's just me and Campsey now. I came here to settle with him and nothing is going to stop me. Been living for it these many years."

"Alright, been nice knowin' you."

I began my walk toward Shannon, he began his toward me, and then we were about thirty-five feet apart. I already knew the words, as I had uttered them thousands of times before, so I spoke them.

"You and your Regulators murdered my father. Remember that? Then, you watched as your brother Wyley took a whip to me. Now I'm with the law. You can come willing with me and the marshal or else you can make a mistake. Your call. But I'm hoping I get to ventilate you."

Well, you should've seen that look of pure rage appear on the face of Shannon Campsey. It was a thing of pure beauty, I've got to say. He reached down toward his right holster, grabbed, took too sudden of an aim and fired. Right as he squeezed the trigger he fell to the ground, lifeless, one of his now dead eyes to the right of the bullet entry, the other to the left. Adams walked up alongside me and we stared down at the body.

"That looked easy, Frank. Way too easy. He drew and fired at you first, and he was fast. He played hell."

"Which one is next on our list?"

"Well, my informants tell me that Doc Ferber spends a lot of time over near California Creek. He's one of the Regulators you're after, and the ride there will only take about a day. He's wanted for cattle rustling by Cherokee officials."

"Sounds good to me. Doc will hold second place on our list of distinguished gentlemen. My stepfather has a few Cherokee friends over near California Creek. Maybe we can go visit them. Maybe they have seen him recently and can give us exact whereabouts."

"Eaton, I gotta ask you. For a few moments in that fracas with Shannon, you acted like you had done that a thousand times."

"I've done it more than a thousand times."

"Whataya mean?"

"A thousand times in my mind."

8

We got to the vicinity of California Creek and located the cabin of one of my stepfather's Cherokee friends. We spent a few hours with him and he provided some good information. He gave us information relative to Doc and he mentioned that John Ferber, Doc's brother, was in Southwest City, Missouri, tending bar, running a faro table, rustling cattle, and running with skunks.

We scouted the country around California Creek for a good day before running across any sign. The sign came in the form of the smell of singed cowhide floating on the wind. Curious, we followed the smell. In no time, we came across just the kind of scene I was hoping for.

From behind our perch in the trees, we spied two men branding cattle. One of the men I had never seen before, but the other one was a man whose face I would never forget — Doc Ferber! Just as before, a fear began welling up in my gut as I thought about the bullets that were about to fly and the bodies that were about to drop, and how one of those bodies could be mine. Again, I thought about sweet Adelita, and how much better it would be holding her hand, stealing kisses and holding her soft womanly body instead of dodging bullets with the likes of a hardened murderer like Doc Ferber.

Doc looked about as I remembered him, just older and more haggard. Of course, that didn't bother me none. He had called the play a long time ago and I just came to finish the job thereof. As for the other fellow, even though I didn't know him I still knew he was trouble by the looks of his Regulator-style dress. He wore the wide-brimmed sombrero, the colorful bandana, the near knee-high boots adorned with devil and death tarot cards, and the flashy silver spurs. He was Regulator through and through and that meant he was as dangerous as any scorpion or rattlesnake.

Anyways, I told Adams that one of those fellows was Doc Ferber for sure. I could tell that by the patch he wore over his eye. We decided to ride up peaceable-like.

We came out from behind the trees with

our mounts keeping a slow, steady walk. We caught them both unaware. Doc was down on his knees tending to a steer but, once he saw us, got up quick and cupped his right palm over the butt of his pistol, saying, "Who the hell are ya'll?"

Adams wanted to make sure we did this thing the law and order way, and so he was the first to respond.

"I'm Chris Adams, U.S. Marshal out of Fort Smith working for Judge Parker. We want to question you for possible cattle rustle rustling."

"Oh, is that right? You both look like you sit in the front pew at church."

Then Doc looked over to me, personal-like.

"Who are you? What are you doing here and what in the hell do you want?"

Doc sure was perplexed by me, like he had seen me somewhere before. I wasn't wearing a badge yet, either, and that probably confused him some.

About that time, Adams' horse got spooked over something, reared up and then dropped him on the ground directly in front of Doc. Adams tried to rise to both feet but his injured leg kept him from standing up quick enough to avoid Doc grabbing him and placing the barrel of his sidearm firmly against his temple. Adams' eyes got as big as silver dollars and the sweat started streaming down his face as he realized just what a damned fine predicament he had gotten himself into. I didn't know what we were going to do at this point either, but my mind started working the problem over full bore because Doc and his friend were now in complete control of the situation. Doc wasn't going to let us forget it, either. He looked straight at me.

"You there! Drop your weapons or else your friend here gets his brains blown out. Drop your pieces, both of them."

Well, I got to tell you, I was some scared to death on the inside at the damned fix we now found ourselves in. My brain was sort of addled at that time, but there was one thing I knew and knew for sure: I could not turn over my weapons at that point or else Adams and I both were going to die for sure on a beautiful day out there along California Creek in the Cherokee Nation of the Indian Territory. That was wisdom straight from the gut, and I wasted no time stating my case.

"I turn over nothing. You blow his head off and you lose yours. You're an easy target at this distance, and I like my chances of ventilating you after you do for my badge friend here."

About that time, Doc's friend chimed in.

"Don't forget about me. I make sure that regardless of what happens you die any damned way, savvy?"

All of this was giving Adams to think his minutes were numbered and I was thinking he might be right.

"For God's sake, Frank! Do as they say!"

"No deal, Doc. Go ahead and kill the badge there. No skin off my ass. Just know this — by the time he hits the ground you're just as dead as him. And your friend is right behind you."

"Frank, please drop your guns. This is insanity!"

All to once, Doc's friend got a curious look on his face, looked to me, and started asking questions.

"Mister, just what is it you want?"

"I just want Doc Ferber there, and I'm sure glad I've found him."

"Frank! Frank! God Almighty. They'll kill me!"

Looking straight at me, Doc tightened his hold on Adams and jammed that gun barrel harder into his temple — real violent-like. Of course, poor Adams was scared to death and I would have been, too. Adams' face showed cold, dead fear and his words were spoken at a lower pitch now, almost at a whisper, as if he was starting to accept a certain death.

"Frank. Frank . . ."

Doc pressed the gun barrel harder against Adams' head and continued his gaze toward me.

"Who the hell are you, anyhow? And how do you know who I am?"

"I am Frank Eaton and I ought to know you, Doc Ferber, for you are one of the men who killed my father! You son of a bitch!"

Well, old Doc Ferber acted as if he had been belted in the belly with an axe handle. He was sure shocked! He had that good left eye of his wide open and his mouth was ajar. He was face to face with the son of the man he had helped gun down so many years before and he was some astonished. Using the same hand holding his pistol, he reached up to straighten his eye patch.

And that was his mistake.

As soon as he raised his hand to the eye patch, I drew both of my sidearms and they belched fire. In one slick, oily motion, I had brought Doc to the ground with a hole to his forehead and then blasted the rifle from his friend's grip before he could whirl it around to fire. As I kept my guns on Doc's friend, I walked over and looked down at the body of the fallen Regulator just to make sure he was good and dead.

"Yours was the first rattle out of the box, Doc. But you didn't dig fast enough, you poor bastard!"

Then I turned my attention to Doc's friend.

"We're appropriating these cattle you've stolen and we're taking them back to the Cherokees from whence they came. We'll look past the rustling for now, but this will be the last time I look past you. Ride!"

"Why you lettin' me go?"

"I don't recall you were with the men who killed my father."

The fellow took on a thoughtful look as he mounted his horse and then he looked to me.

"So you're the son of that filthy son of a bitch named Eaton from Kansas, are you?"

"So they say."

"I hope you know what you just did."

"Yeah, I just ventilated one of the low-life curs who murdered my father."

"You just called down the thunder, boy! The Regulators ain't just the Campseys and the Ferbers like it was up in Kansas. No sir! There's a passel of us now. Upwards to sixty. We call the shots in this part of the territory."

"The hell you say."

"The hell I do say. When Shannon got down to the Indian Nations, he recruited a small army of us. You just lit the fuse on a keg o' powder, boy!"

"Well, you can tell the rest of your murdering band of bastards that Shannon Campsey is dead."

Right then, the fellow stared right through me with a look of silent, cold, controlled rage.

"Since when?"

"Since just a few days ago when he drew down on me. Ventilated him. Why don't you draw down on me like Shannon and Doc did? Why don't you draw right now?"

"Not today, Frank Eaton. Not today. But your day is coming. I'm Doyle Campsey and I'm Shannon's brother and you just called it up!"

"Doyle, huh? Well dig for it, Doyle. Bring it right now!"

"That'd be doin' you a favor. Oh no, boy. You done brought it down on the Regulators and we'll deal with you our own way."

Doyle turned his attention to Adams who had been trying to gather himself from the ordeal of a few minutes earlier.

"You there, badge! You with this murderin' scum when he killed my brother?"

"Yep. Fair fight. Your brother drew first and then took lead before he could squeeze the trigger."

"We Regulators have never taken on the law directly before, but you'd better know that's changed now. We'll get the both of you when you least expect it, hear? We're comin'!"

Doyle Campsey rode off to the westward and I couldn't help but wonder when our paths would cross again. I knew I had pissed off a gun-toting rattlesnake that day. I can't say I had ever seen a man as mad as him. He had talked about how the Regulators had grown to a much bigger band of criminals since the night of father's death. I didn't know how true that was. I just wanted the men who gunned down father. I figured I had no beef with anyone else. Someone else could deal with the rest of them yellow-bellied bastards. Adams and I watched Doyle ride off until we were certain he had high-tailed it.

"God Almighty, Frank! You about got me killed!"

"Had I dropped my weapons like Doc wanted we would have both been shot full of holes just then."

Adams dusted off his clothes and managed to compose himself s bit more. He'd sure enough had enough that day.

"You heard what that Doyle Campsey just said. You admitted you killed his brother. You ready to take on an army of mad wolves?"

"I've no issue with their army, just the Campseys and Ferbers, the men who killed father."

"Well you've borrowed more trouble whether you like it or not. It won't be that easy. Not now. They'll have men scouring the country looking for you — and me. And something else. I don't exactly think your way of getting men is what Judge Parker intends, what with the way you push 'em just so's you can draw down on 'em."

"I do something wrong?"

'That's not the kind of law and order needed in the Indian Territory and that's not how Judge Parker has us marshals operate. Leastways, I wouldn't want to be in your boots now, fast or not."

I didn't understand why Adams was saying all of this. I figured he surely understood what a mean bunch of scorpions these Regulators were. That, and he had surely dealt with others in the Indian Territory just as bad and maybe some who were worse. In those days, Indian Territory ran long on folks what'd ventilate you as to look at you, and for the slightest reason or for no reason at all. Leastways, I just let Adams' words go in one ear and out the other. Years later, when I told people the story, there were folks who said that maybe Adams was jealous. I just never could figure out for what reason. Leastways, at the time, I figured I could just as well hunt Regulators on my own with no help, and I told Adams as much.

"You don't have to be a part of this. I'll go it alone if needs must."

"It ain't like that. I'm with ya, Frank. But you're alone for now. I have business back in Fort Smith to handle. You can come with me if you want or wait 'til I get back. Your call."

"What do you have to do in Fort Smith?"

"I'm going to the courthouse to get you papers on the rest of those Regulators if they have them, and I believe they do. We'll have papers to show and that'll make me feel a lot better about this thing."

"I'm not waiting on you. I'm hitting the trail."

"To where?"

"Missouri, just as soon as I get these few head of stolen cattle to someone hereabouts who knows where they belong. Going after John Ferber, Doc's brother. We were just told he is in Southwest City, tending bar, dealing cards and messing around in the business of stolen cattle."

"Have it your way. Just so's you know, I think you're going to get dry gulched. Same for me more than likely cause it looks like we've called it down with the wrong bunch."

"Where can I find you for those papers if I decide I need them?"

"I'll get the papers and then head back to Tahlequah and hang out there for awhile. Find me there. That's if you make it back from Missouri. Make sure you sleep with one eye open."

Of course, I knew where Tahlequah was. It was the capital city of the Cherokee Nation, and still is.

Adams mounted his horse and was about to take off along the trail but pulled up short before turning to me one more time.

"By week's end, every Regulator within two-hundred miles of here will have our description. You're playing against a stacked deck, and you ain't even got to Wyley Campsey yet. Anytime you wanna give up this death wish just let me know."

Adams turned his mount back around and rode off. As I watched the picture of Adams and his horse getting smaller as they rode away, I couldn't help but ponder all of what he had just said about a death wish.

9

So there I was with two of the six Regulators dead and accounted for and I was feeling just fine with my progress. I figured I had made a damned good start on my list of distinguished gentlemen. John Ferber, supposedly in Southwest City, Missouri, was next on my list of social visits.

But, I would be lying if I told you that I wasn't harboring a lot of fear and misgivings as I thought about the work ahead. After all, Doyle Campsey said I had opened up a hornets' nest when I killed his brother, Shannon, and I wasn't forgetting that Wyley, the other brother, waited out there somewhere, most likely in Albuquerque if the stories were true.

And there was something else. In spite of the growing confidence I was gaining in my pistol skills, a great feeling of dread lurked deep within me, and that dread showed up from time to time in the form of those damned nightmares.

Even after I killed both of them, Doc Ferber and Shannon Campsey showed up in those damned dreams. I guess I learned that just because you kill someone doesn't mean they can't haunt you forever at night when you're asleep.

It was the same kind of nightmares as before. Thunder boomed outside the farmhouse of my youth, while shadows danced along the walls within, a display that was interrupted only when the lightening outside added the illusion of daylight to the darkness.

The sound of thundering hooves drowned out even the cracks of thunder outside, and those pounding hooves always served as the terrifying announcement that the Regulators had arrived. The horses came to a halt and the voice of Shannon Campsey rang out.

"Well now, damn you! You got this comin'! When are you flat-headed blue-bellies gonna learn you don't tangle with Regulators, huh?"

The thunder and lightning outside cracks and booms and altogether it is a deafening racket. Devil and death tarot cards dance across the walls and ceiling and into this whole mess enters the image of Wyley

Campsey, and he always repeats those same words.

"Your day is comin', and it's comin' damn soon."

I always see the six horsemen sitting their mounts outside, too. There's Jim, Jonce, Shannon and Wyley Campsey along with John and Doc Ferber. Atop their horses they sit, each of the murdering bastards adorned in all of their Regulator get up.

Then everything becomes hazy and smoky and all I hear is the boom of gunfire and the pounding of hooves as the Regulators escape back into the dark snaky pit that is their home for sure.

As I made my way along the trail to Missouri, I knew in my craw that those Regulators were already scouring a good part of the Indian Territory looking for an opportunity to dry gulch, bushwhack, or skyline me. Now, I didn't know just yet if Doyle was speaking true about their band being a small army, as that could have been so much bluster.

Anyhow, I knew better than to let a guard down in my travels. Regardless of the actual number of Regulators scattered about, I knew I was now a target. I knew Doyle had already alerted his network of murderers of my description, and they had probably watched some of my movements already.

In times such as those — hell, most anytime — it was smart to watch your back trail and live with fireless camps at night. Campfires attract company, and I wasn't looking for any.

Another reason to avoid campfires at night, whether you're on the dodge or on the prowl, is because they can blind you to the goings-on in and around your camp. You sit there looking into the fire for a spell, as is the way with we humans, and then you're blinded for several moments when you look away. That's dangerous. It's sort of like making camp near a rushing stream. The sound of that rushing water keeps you from hearing what's going on around you. You had to be aware of those kinds of things while on the trail in those days, especially when you were up against the kind of yellow-bellied snakes that I was right then. Hell, truth be told, it pays to be smart like that these days.

Anyhow, I knew those dry gulching, gut robbing Regulators would be looking for just those kind of opportunities to come up on me unawares. No sir, I determined to watch my business and keep that from happening.

From where I started in the Cherokee Nation of the Indian Territory, it was just a hop, skip and jump to Southwest City, Missouri, a town so named because of its far southwesterly location in that state. The little berg sits just a short distance beyond the eastern border of the Indian Territory.

All of the information collected in the territory gave me to believe John Ferber waited at the end of the trail in Southwest City where he owned an interest in a saloon and worked in rustled cattle, an endeavor familiar to all those damned Regulators.

I crossed Honey Creek and rode up to the edge of Southwest City as the sun went down. After pulling up short of the town and deliberating for a few minutes, I decided to take cover in the woods adjoining the town and let darkness drape the countryside a bit more before making myself known to the folks thereabouts. From my perch in the woods, I could see one saloon lining the little main street. Lantern lights glowed from the inside and the boisterous voices of those within gave me to know a good time was being had by one and all. Laughter and cursing rang out, coins rattled on the poker tables, bar maids shrieked as men pinched their bottoms, and someone knocked out a lively tune on the piano.

I walked Bo up to the street in front of the saloon and loosely tied him off, making sure to tie him off-center of the front saloon door. I didn't want any stray bullets bringing down my means of escape if I had to leave town muy pronto, and the chances were good that I would need to.

I walked up to the door of the saloon and stood there a spell. I wanted to see if I could spot that bastard named John Ferber before ambling on in. I had a picture of all of those Regulators in my mind, and I still do to this day. You just don't forget the appearances of those who gun down your father in such a cowardly way. I was looking for a man with a heavily cultivated and waxed mustache wearing all the trappings of a Regulator — the decorated boots, the fancy sword, and a belt shining with those silver conchos. From my spot at the door, I didn't see anyone fitting that exact description, so I determined to go on in and ask some questions that might help me locate my man.

To be honest, my belly fluttered to beat the band I was so nervous, just as it had on the two previous confrontations, but I had it to do, so I walked on into the ring.

No sooner had I broke the threshold of the doorway did I notice two heavily-armed pistoleros standing near the far wall, one to the left and the other to the right. I had never seen either of the two before, but they both wore those high-topped boots decorated with devil and death tarot cards with their britches tucked inside the boots so everyone could see the pretty artwork. They both took a good look at me, sizing me up from top to bottom. One nodded to the other as if to say, "Yeah, that's our man." That's when both of them disappeared through doorways at each of the opposite corners of the saloon. That had me some worried. I don't like it when I can't see men who look like they might dry-gulch me on the spot.

Boy, it was a lively scene inside. There were men drinking at the main bar and at small tables scattered throughout the room, there were poker tables filled with folks looking to beat the house, and there were pretty ladies with nearly bare bottoms darting this way and that. At the center of the room, six men minded their hands at a card table that seemed like the main center of attention. A fancy dressed fellow smoking a thin cigar was the dealer and, for some reason, he looked like he might be in charge of the whole shooting match. Standing by him was a right pretty buxom blonde adorned in all the saloon girl trappings — high heels, see-through lace hose, and clothing throughout that showed a man just what she was made of. And, while there was no arguing that she sized up just right, I was trying to keep my eyes on other things in that saloon, like where everyone sat, whose rifles and sidearms were ready to hand, and the location of all doors and opened windows.

The dealer smoking the thin cigar looked up to me.

"Something I can help you with, son?"

"I was just looking for some information."

"Just information?"

"Truth be told, I'm looking for a man I heard might be in town, and who might even work here. Man by the name of John Ferber."

Well, those last two words served to get everybody's attention. I mean you could've heard a pin drop right about then. Everyone in the saloon turned their attention to me and gave me the damnedest stares. Buxom blonde, she gave me a look that seemed to say, "Get out of this saloon while you have the chance because you just lit the fuse on the fireworks."

Right about then, the dealer took a puff from that thin cigar, slapped buxom blonde on her almost bare ass and told her to go get us two glasses of whiskey. The table stood nearby that held a stack of whiskey glasses and a bottle, so she didn't have to go far to fulfill his request.

"Son, you got a lot of nerve coming in here asking questions like that. Why are you looking for John Ferber?"

Real quick-like, buxom blonde had returned to the table with a bottle and two glasses in hand.

"I want John Ferber because he ran with a passel of curs what shot my father down in cold blood. Called themselves Regulators."

"I heard of them Regulators. When did this happen?"

"When I was a kid of a boy back in southeast Kansas."

One of the card players, a thin, elderly man sporting a bald head, spoke up.

"Was your father a man by the name of Eaton?"

"He was."

"Had a farm and a boarding house right there on the Santa Fe Trail?"

"Like I said, mister. That was him."

"Remember it well. Murdered by those damned Regulators. Called themselves Southerners, and still do, but Lee and Jackson would have been the first to order them son of a bitches shot."

The dealer gave the old man a disapproving glance.

"Careful, there's some right here in this joint who claim to run with that bunch."

Then the dealer looked up at me.

"And you might do well to remember that, as well."

I took a sip of my whiskey, looked around the saloon a little more to further size up the lay of the land, and spied a couple of fellows at a nearby card table who wore those devil and death boots with their jeans tucked inside. Counting those two pistoleros who slithered away when they seen me come in, that made four men here who most likely considered themselves Regulators. And I damned sure wasn't forgetting those two pistoleros what had slunk off. My mind kept calculating where they might be.

In the meantime, buxom blonde kept giving me the strangest look, and I couldn't quite figure out why.

"So, mister dealer, what do you know in the way of a certain John Ferber, former Regulator and one of the six who bore my father full of holes like he was a damned rag doll?"

"Son, John Ferber was shot and killed in this very place just last night."

Well, I got to tell you, that bit of news hit me like a load of bricks, and I was concerned about whether to believe it or not.

"What? I don't get it."

"Let's put it this way. John Ferber wasn't very good at dealing a one-eyed jack off the bottom of the deck. He's gonna be buried outside town in a grave dug on the quick."

"I want to see the body."

"Why do you want to see the body?"

"I made a vow I'd track down every last one of father's murderers and even the score. If John Ferber is dead then so be it, but I ain't leaving town until I see his body."

"There's a one-room shack at the far end of town. You'll find his body in there. The door is unlocked. Just walk on in."

I looked up from the dealer and made ready to leave the building, but I had been listening to his words so closely that I didn't notice those two fellows with the devil and death boots had gotten up from their table and were standing right in front of me. They were Regulators for sure, what with all of their fancy trappings. They both had the cultivated mustaches, twirled at the ends, and I could tell they thought pretty highly of themselves. The one to my left, the smartest looking of the two, spoke up first.

"So, you're the son of that Eaton our boys finished up in Kansas some years back?"

"That's the rumor."

The two exchanged smiling glances with each other, as if to say that easy fun was ahead.

"We've heard all about that pa of yours. Heard he was nothin' but a low-life Yankee coward."

Inside, I was seething with anger over what was said about father, but I wasn't going to let either of them see it. I just smiled and let the talkative one keep on talking.

"Boy, what makes you think you could've handled our friend, John?"

"Why couldn't I? I already did for his brother, Doc. Then I did for Shannon Campsey, your murdering leader, after that. Ventilated both of them sonsabitches, just like I'm about to ventilate the both of you, right here, right now if that's what you want."

"Boy, you ain't making it out of this saloon, and you ain't going down to see John's body. This is the end of the line for you and you've killed your last Regulator."

About that time, I figured it was my turn to talk, and so I made sure I said a piece.

"I've no issue with either of you two here tonight. I came for John Ferber, to do to him what I've already done with Doc Ferber and Shannon Campsey. But if it's trouble you want I have all you need in spades. You two can both draw down on me first, and I want every man in here to know I said so and to watch you do it."

You couldn't hear a whisper out of anyone right about then. All the folks were quiet and had all their eyes on the two Regulators and me.

"Draw down, I said! Dig!"

Now, I got to tell you something. In my mind's eye, what happened after that just came nice and easy and slow-like. The talkative Regulator drew his sidearm first, but my weapon spit fire before he could fully raise his to bear. As for the quiet one, all I had to do was pivot the business end of my sidearm the least little bit and fire just as he was about to have his weapon raised high enough to do any damage. The result of the affair was two crumpled Regulator bodies on the saloon floor in Southwest City.

It was right in there somewhere that I determined my best course of action would be to get my ass out of there, muy pronto. I planned on backing out of that saloon with my face to those inside, lest there be other Regulators who might try and back shoot me.

"Alright, all you sonsabitches! I'm backing out of here and if anyone so much as looks like they might try for a gun I'm going to ventilate them, hear?"

I made it all the way to the door and was about to step aboard Bo when the flurry of gunfire began. Something, maybe the hair on the back of my neck that started to stand, served as warning, and I darted behind a column in front of the saloon just as the gunfire commenced. That bit of premonition saved my damned life.

From my position behind the wood column, I saw two shadows run across an alley opposite the saloon, but they didn't run for long. Shadowy targets as big as those, and not more than thirty-five feet from me on a moonlit night were all the target I needed with my sidearms still smoking hot from their previous work inside the saloon. Down they both went, their crumpled bodies not three feet from one another.

I ran over to get a look at the bodies and, sure enough, they belonged to the two Regulators who made themselves scarce as soon as I walked in the saloon. I kind of figured they meant to bushwhack me, and, sure enough, they tried.

I topped Bo and proceeded to the shack at the end of the street. I walked inside, lit a match, and saw the cold body of John Ferber laying there looking a helluva lot older than since I had last seen him, and a whole helluva lot deader.

Satisfied, I walked out of the shack, topped Bo and started for the trail back to Indian Territory. All to once, I heard a female voice. I pivoted Bo back around and wouldn't you know it, there was that pretty buxom blonde standing in the middle of the street.

"That's what I was trying to tell you back there. I knew those two would be waiting on you outside to shoot you in the back if they could. Had I said something in there they would've killed me. I'm glad you're alive."

"Thank you. I knew you were trying to tell me something."

"What's your name?"

"The name is Eaton. Frank Eaton."

"So long, Frank Eaton."

"Adios."

That pretty lady walked back to the saloon, looking back a couple of times, while I sat there contemplating all that had happened that night. I crossed the third Regulator off my list of distinguished gentlemen. Sure, I wasn't the one who evened the score. Someone else, and I know not whom, took care of that for me, and I had to kill four men to find out.

I started for the trail again at a damn good clip, and this time I didn't look back.

10

My next destination was the town of Tahlequah back down in the Cherokee Nation of the Indian Territory. There, I would wait for my partner, Chris Adams. Adams said to hole up there and wait for him, as he would have papers on the remaining bunch of Regulators we were after. Them sonsabitches were wanted for all kinds of assorted crimes, mostly cattle rustling. I'll be honest, I didn't care a damn if I had legal papers on them or not. I had a score to settle and I planned on getting it done. I was just trying to abide by the spirit of our partnership, so to speak, as that is what men do who go in cahoots.

Come daylight the day following the shootout in the Southwest City saloon, I woke up from a night's rest, looked down at my right side and saw blood. I'll be damned if I didn't get grazed by one of those assassins waiting for me out in the street. My heart was pounding too hard and everything was going too fast during that fracas for me to notice. I tried to stand up and discerned right off that there was a soreness in my side that limited my movements way too much for my liking. Like it or not, I knew I had to hole up somewhere and fight of shy people until I was limber again.

For the next few days, I remained hidden in a tight grove of trees along a bend of Honey Creek and thought things over. All kinds of thoughts meandered through my brain. I thought of the remaining three men on my list — Jim, Jonce and Wyley Campsey, brothers to one another and each of them no better than any copperhead snake or water moccasin.

Then there was Doyle, their other brother. For some reason his likeness kept returning to my mind's eye. Doyle spoke as if he was the head Regulator now, and that's because I had ventilated his brother, Shannon, the former leader. Doyle said he had himself an army of about sixty men these days, and my mind couldn't help but constantly see a massive cluster of such men storming across the countryside with one goal in mind — ridding the world of me.

I had heard Jim and Jonce Campsey were working rustled cattle in the Ozark foothills in the Cherokee Nation. The story was that the two ran together, and I sure hoped that was true. I figured it made better use of my time to find the two of them together. My plan was to wait on Adams in Tahlequah and then we would hit the trail for Jim and Jonce.

I thought a lot of Adelita. She never really left my thoughts. I knew I needed to get this Regulator business finished so I could be with her. She said she wanted me to come with her and live the life of a gypsy, and I was some inclined to do just that. She was the sweetest, the most beautiful and the most mysterious woman I had ever known, and to imagine spending the rest of my life by her side made me feel as if there was some good still left in a world that had dealt me and mine some bad cards. Evening the score with these Regulators was an ugly business, and thinking about Adelita made everything seem a whole helluva lot better.

Of course, them horrible dreams stayed with me of a night. It was an irksome thing to me that Wyley Campsey had set up business in my head for all those many years, always reminding me that he was going to kill me, always repeating how my time was coming. I lived with that sonsabitch day in and day out, and I couldn't help but think about how the final showdown with him would play out. I wanted it over with.

After resting for a few days, and allowing the pain in my side to fizzle, I hit the trail for Tahlequah. I was ready to be among townies again, to sleep in a soft bed at the National Hotel and eat delicious square meals at Aunt Taylor's place. I had been in Tahlequah before, and carried fond memories of the Cherokee people there and of their warm hospitality.

On our way to Tahlequah, Bo and me were just a few miles north of the town, following a trail that skirted the Illinois River, when I spied something that I never in my wildest dreams expected to see.

Sitting right there along the banks of the river not a hundred yards from me were the three vardo caravans that belonged to my sweet Adelita and her family. I could recognize enough of the family members to know that I had, sure enough, happened upon Adelita once again. It was a grand day!

Even though Adelita's people traveled the country constantly, never staying in one place too long, which increased the chances of a traveling man like me to run into them, I still counted myself lucky to see Adelita again. There was no other reason but good fortune that I found myself in her midst once more.

Adelita's cousin, Stevo, kept giving me the evil eye every time I stood close and visited with her. Adelita's grandmother was polite and friendly, but I had always gotten the feeling she didn't care for me none, and I got that feeling again this time. Altogether, though, her family seemed happy to see me again, and we made merry that first night just as we had done the last time I ran across them. There was music and food and fun around the big campfire that evening. Adelita and me danced the flamenco again and I was sure proud that I had not forgotten the moves and steps she had taught me before. I was a regular gypsy dancer!

Adelita and me never left each other's side, and Stevo kept an eye on our every move. Jealousy was written all over his face but I didn't care none at all.

I slept in my bedroll near the vardos that night, enjoying the campfire as it went from being a pit of roaring flames to nothing but glowing red embers. When I awoke the next morning, I stepped down to a spot in the river where the water ran clean and clear and freshened up a bit.

Later, Adelita stepped out of her vardo, went down to the river behind a cluster of brush and scrub trees, and did the same.

Then, she went back inside her vardo to fix her hair and such, and when she came back out I could've swore she was the most beautiful female who had ever lived.

I asked her if she wanted to go into Tahlequah and have dinner later that day at Aunt Taylor's and she said that would be just fine. I could tell the idea tickled her. She said that most of the meals of her life were eaten beside a campfire and that sitting down to a dinner table in town would be, to her, a great luxury. When she said that I was some glad I brought up the subject.

We rode into Tahlequah just in time for the mid-day meal at Aunt Taylor's. Son, I will surely never forget all the looks my sweet Adelita got from the townies thereabouts. She was the center of attention that day and I was some proud she was with me. By the time we entered town and tied reins in front of the restaurant, I'll bet fifty different people had cast awe struck gazes her way.

When we walked into Aunt Taylor's it was more of the same. Every eye in the place focused on Adelita. It was like those folks had never seen a woman who looked as beautiful and mysterious as her. And, I agreed with them.

We sat down to table and Adelita was sure enough happy to be there. I couldn't help but think of all the happy times that we would have together in the future. She told me her folks had been pressuring her to marry Stevo, and I told her I would come for her just as soon as I had finished evening the score with the remaining Regulators.

"How many more are there?"

"There's three of them — Jim, Jonce and Wyley Campsey."

"Where are these men?"

"Jim and Jonce are around here close by, I'm told. Somewhere in these Ozark foothills."

"Let these men go and come with me."

"It won't be long until I come for you and put all matters to rest. Just hang on. Where will you be? I mean, will your folks stay around Tahlequah for long?"

"We're starting for Albuquerque soon, my grandfather says."

"That's where Wyley is supposed to be, too. The cards of the past ring true, Adelita. Albuquerque is in those cards just as you said before. Why does your grandfather want to see that place?"

"He wants to see the El Camino Real de Tierra Adentro."

"What's that?"

"The Royal Road. Grandfather says we have Spanish ancestors who came up from Mexico City along that trail. He wants to see it before his time is gone."

"And it goes through Albuquerque?"

"Yes, and then north to Santa Fe."

So, just as Adelita's cards had said before, it sure looked as if Adelita and me would soon see each other again out in New Mexico. I'd be looking for Wyley Campsey and she would be with her folks living life out on the gypsy trail.

Right about then, a loud commotion reached our ears from outside Aunt Taylor's. There was loud voices, yelling and whinnying horses. I got up forthwith and headed outside. Adelita waited for me at the doorway where she stood watch.

Out in the street in front of the old courthouse a crowd of men had gathered around the back end of a buckboard where they examined something laying within. Once I reached the buckboard, I saw what they were looking at. It was the mangled, tortured and almost unrecognizable body of Marshal Chris Adams. My partner had been tortured in the most horrible way and then killed. A fiery hatred welled up inside of me as I thought of what had been done to my friend, and especially as I pondered those who had surely done it.

I looked up to the buckboard driver and told him I knew the man he had just wheeled into town. He answered with a question.

"Is your name Frank Eaton?"

"Yes, how did you know?"

"The fellow laying there described you before he died."

"Where did you find him?"

"Back along the trail from Fort Smith. He was just barely alive when I found him, though."

"I hope he told you who did this."

"He mentioned a Doyle Campsey. Something about Regulators. Asked me to reach inside his coat pocket for these papers here. Said they are from Judge Parker's office and to give them to you."

"He say anything else?"

"Just to get him to Tahlequah and to look you up. I've never seen such a thing as this."

"Killing a man is one thing, but this is the work of devil curs, murdering hell hounds like them Regulators."

"Oh, he said something else. Said he had it on good authority from folks at the courthouse in Fort Smith that Wyley Campsey is in Albuquerque, New Mexico. Said to tell you. I'm glad you're here so I can honor this man's wish."

I turned to walk away and ran into an elderly Cherokee man, a man who looked as if he had forgotten more of life's secrets than I might ever know. His face showed the wisdom of years and his voice spoke of great knowledge but also of humility and understanding.

"Are you the Frank Eaton who trails the men who killed his father many years ago?"

I nodded yes.

"Everyone has heard of your story, of the unspeakable thing that happened to your father in Kansas that night. We have heard of your great skill with the pistols, of your speed and of your accuracy. We have heard of your courage and of how you live to fulfill the pledge you made to your father's friend to avenge this great wrong."

"What is your name, old man?"

"My name is not important right now. What is important is you go to that woman who looks from the doorway. This woman loves you with the force of a great river, and such love is not found but once in a man's life. Go to her and leave this terrible business behind you. Leave it forever. The men who call themselves Regulators will do the same to you that they did to your father and to the man in the wagon."

"I respect your words, and I can't say you aren't right, because you more than likely are. I just can't turn away from a job that I'm beholdin' to finish, especially after what just happened to my friend here."

The old man knew I had spoken my piece and he offered no reply. But, there was a look on his face that seemed even stronger and wiser than his words to me. He slowly walked away and I never crossed paths with him again. I remember his face to this very day.

As I watched the old Cherokee man make his way across the dirt street of Tahlequah, the buckboard driver walked over and handed me a piece of paper.

"This was pinned to your friend's chest when I found him."

On the paper, I read the words, "A nosey Parker who hunted the wrong men."

Those words filled me with a rage I couldn't control. Those words came from cur dogs that held themselves above the law, and I had seen enough of their work.

There were about forty or so men standing around the buckboard. I climbed atop it and spoke to all of them and anyone else within earshot.

"I want everyone to hear me out. Especially to any Regulators or friends of Regulators who are here right now. My name is Frank Eaton and I have been on the trail to even the score with the men who gunned down my father like a mangy cur. I've three to settle with before that score is settled — those would be Jim, Jonce and Wyley Campsey. Then, I'm doing for their brother Doyle for what happened to Marshal Chris Adams here. He was my partner and wanted nothing more than to bring some kind of law to this country. I'll find the sonsabitch and do my friend right. I'll ventilate any Regulator who gets in my way. Spread the word."

After that, I walked over to have words with Adelita. I told her all about what happened. I told her who that was laying dead in the buckboard and what had happened to him. I told her that man was my partner and that he had been brutally tortured and killed while helping me trail the men who killed father.

I escorted Adelita back to her family's camp by the river. I explained to her family all that had happened that day and how I had to hit the trail for Jim, Jonce, Wyley and now Doyle Campsey. I said my adieus to Adelita and pledged to her that I would make quick work of it.

Even so, I rode away as the tears streamed down her beautiful face.

11

Jim and Jonce Campsey, the men fourth and fifth on my list of distinguished gentlemen, presented themselves to me in dramatic fashion just a few days after I left Tahlequah in search of them.

"Seek and ye shall find," someone once told me. Son, that saying sure proved out for me in the case of Jim and Jonce out there in the middle of them Ozark foothills on a beautiful day in Cherokee Nation of the Indian Territory. I figured to be on the trail for weeks searching for these buzzards, but I was sure glad I was wrong.

I made it a practice in those days to occasionally bring Bo to a halt, stand up in the stirrups, and then let my senses go to work. I would look off in every direction and comb the landscape section by section for any interesting sign. I could also hear better with Bo at a halt because there was no creaking saddle leather and clip-clop of horse hooves to hinder my hearing.

But, it wasn't my eyes or my ears that led me to my intended prey that day. It was my nose.

The scent I caught was just a slight one at first, and almost undetectable, but I knew I had caught wind of something sure enough. I factored the wind direction and soon surmised the smell came from somewhere northwest of my location. So, that's the direction in which I rode. Sure as hell, the further northwest we went, the stronger was the smell — the smell of burnt cowhide.

Soon, I found myself in a great forest of oak and hickory with a lot of underbrush. I sure didn't see how anyone would be branding cattle in such an area, but I stayed with my senses and kept to the scent.

Sure enough, after traipsing almost a mile through the hardwood, Bo and me came to a spot where I saw the forest's edge ahead, a clearing beyond, and a group of men.

I had a bad premonition about it.

All to once, the hair on the back of my neck stood straight up and my heart began pounding so hard that I could hear the boom in my ears. I tied Bo off well back in the trees and began slowly making my way toward the clearing. My aim was to stay hidden all the way to the clearing and present myself only if and when I chose to.

Turned out, I had waltzed right down upon one hell of a shindig. From a well-hidden position behind a massive oak tree, I peeked out beyond the trees and into the open area. Out there in that clearing, just at the edge of the forest, not thirty-five feet from me, was Jim and Jonce Campsey, sitting in their saddles, with their sidearms on a group of four Cherokee cattlemen and one white man who had been branding cattle. The scent of singed cowhide hung heavy in the air, and I was sure glad I caught wind of it when I did.

Jim and Jonce hadn't changed too awfully much in the years since father's death. They both donned the wide sombreros typical of them damned Regulators, the leather bedecked in all those silver conchos and those flashy high-topped devil and death boots. They still wore the thick mustaches, twirled at the ends, and the goatees. Jim's hair had a reddish tint while Jonce's ran more to blonde. All of them damned Campseys had a sort of look about them. I'd grown to loathe it.

Jim dismounted and proceeded to plant the business end of his pistol firmly against the temple of one of the Cherokees who was still in the kneeling position for branding cattle. I figured I must've got there in the nick of time, just when the action had commenced.

Jonce kept his sorry ass up in the saddle while Jim did all the talking.

"Howe many times do we Regulators have to tell ya, huh?"

The Cherokee cattleman stayed in his kneeling position and I could tell he was too damned terrified to talk.

"These are Regulator cattle and you stole them. Ain't that right, Red Bird?"

I knew I had heard of a man named Red Bird, a fellow associated with a group of Cherokees wanting to fight the rustling going on back in those days.

The man named Red Bird stayed perfectly still and mumbled something in Cherokee to his fellow cattlemen. Jim wasn't too happy with that.

"What's that?"

There was no response from Red Bird or from anyone in his group.

"I'm gonna ask one more damned time and someone better tell me what you just said or else I'm gonna kill one of your friends here! What'd you say?"

"I said I know you are going to kill us."

"Oh, you do, do you? Stand up, you son of a bitch!"

Red Bird remains motionless.

Right about then, Jim rams that gun barrel even harder into Red Bird's temple, nearly knocking him over. Jim keeps up with the yelling.

Red Bird didn't move a muscle.

"When I tell you to do something I damned well mean for you to do it, savvy?"

Red Bird remained almost perfectly still with his mouth agape. He was as terrified as any man I had ever seen. His face gleamed with sweat, and I knew his heart must've been pounding like a hammer.

The other three Cherokees, on whom Jonce still had his sidearm pointed, looked ashamed that they couldn't do anything to help their friend. They exchanged glances with Red Bird and the whole thing was a dangerous and horrible spectacle. Up until that time, I was hesitant to show myself for fear that Jim would pull that trigger and send Red Bird to beyond the veil. That's about the time Red Bird spoke up.

"I will gladly die than lick your boots."

"Hear that, Jonce? Red Bird, here — he thinks he's a brave one. You don' think he's trying to call our bluff, do you? Red Bird, you trying to call our bluff?"

That's when Jim Campsey laughed this despicable laugh. The laugh gave me to know the Regulator had reached his end and was on the verge of crossing the line into something far more evil. Red Bird must've felt the same way. By this time, the beads of sweat rolled down the Cherokee's face like a waterfall as he fought to control the trembling of his body. Jim Campsey rammed that gun barrel harder against his temple and slowly cocked his piece. The click sounded like a lightning crack.

I walked out into the open and introduced myself, the barrel of one of my sidearms on Jim, and the other on Jonce. Jim had his back to me, as did Jonce who was still sitting his horse.

"Holster it, Jim! Right damned now! You, too Jonce!"

Well, you could've heard a pin drop about that time. Both of those Campseys slowly turned around to see their new visitor, and I had never see two men look so befuddled, and those four Cherokees looked some relieved. It was a beautiful sight to behold, and I was some proud of myself for living long enough to be there at that time and place.

Both Campseys froze all movement, not even blinking their eyes. Jim was frozen so stiff he hadn't even holstered his pistol like I told him to.

"Jim, I told you to put that sidearm back in its sheath. Holster it now or else I'll ventilate the both of you!"

He slowly slid the piece back into its holster.

"Now, Jim, I want you to turn and face me. Jonce, get down off that horse and do the same. Both of you get those hands in the air."

They did as I told them. Jim was the first to muster any words.

"Just holster them? You don't want us to drop them on the ground?"

"That's right. You're going to need those pistols."

"Who the hell are you?"

"Oh, Jim, I think you know me."

I could see the wheels turning in Jonce's head right before he figured out my identity.

"I know who he is, Jim. It's an Eaton, son of that blue belly up in Kansas we killed. I figure he's wantin' the same as his daddy got."

Jim chimed in.

"Heard you murdered our brother, Shannon. Is that right?"

"Well, you boys do know me. Yes, I evened the score with your brother, just like I'm going to even the score with both of you, right here, right now. Then, I'm hitting the trail for that other brother of yours, Wyley."

Jim and Jonce both looked at each other and smiled like they were in on some damned secret. Jim kept talking.

"You won't find him. Not that it matters. He'd kill you if you did."

"Boys, I know Wyley has left this part of the country and is now in Albuquerque tending bar and dealing in rustled cattle."

That bit of information caught them both in the gut and they gave each other a look indicating they were surprised at hearing it. Maybe they had been thinking no one knew of Wyley's whereabouts.

"I know more than you think. I hear a lot of things from my informants on the trail and from the courthouse in Fort Smith. You see boys, it's all legal when I ventilate the both of you here today. I work for Judge Parker. One of his deputies."

"Makes no difference to Jonce and me. We'd soon kill a badge as the next guy. Just how do you plan on killing us. Fair fight? Maybe one at a time?"

"I'll do you one better. You can both dig at the same time when you're of a mind to. Red Bird, get your folks back out of the way."

Red Bird did as I instructed and it made

me feel better knowing they were out of the way.

"You see, Jim, I'm sure glad I found you two both together here today. This is going to be a two-for-one afternoon."

"Sounds good to me."

"I'm sure it does. But I know you would both prefer I was unarmed with my back to you. Something I need to tell you first, though, before I kill you."

"What's that?"

"Not only did I do for Shannon, but I also ventilated Doc. And Doc's brother, John, well he was killed the night before I could get to him up in Southwest City. You two are fourth and fifth on my list of distinguished gentlemen."

The two exchanged glances again, but this time they both had a more serious look on their faces when they did. I was getting some tired of all the talk and was ready to dance, and I told them so.

"C'mon boys. Now is as good a time as any. Yours can be the first rattle out of the box. Dig!"

Jonce reached for his piece first, Jim second, and only Jonce had time to get a shot off before his body fell to the ground. Jim went down before he brought his sidearm to bear.

The smoke cleared, my heart quit pounding, and the bodies of number four and five lay sprawled before the four Cherokee cattlemen and me. Red Bird walked over and shook my hand with much appreciation.

"Damn, man! That's fast. Never seen such!"

"Save it. A man is always lucky to not come out of one of these deals seriously shot up or, worse, dead."

"I thought we were dead men today. How can we thank you?"

"You can thank me if and when I make it back from New Mexico where I'm going after the brother of these two, the brother who happens to be the fastest one in the family."

"That'd be Wyley Campsey?"

"I guess everyone knows."

"We heard your story, Frank Eaton. Wyley helped these two here steal our cattle before leaving to New Mexico some time ago."

I went back in amongst the oaks and hickory trees and brought Bo in. I was surprised that Red Bird knew Bo's name.

"So this is Bowlegs? Heard of him."

"I call him Bo for short. Seems like you know a lot about me."

"You're making a name for yourself

throughout not only the Cherokee Nation, but even down in the nations of the Choctaws, Creeks, Chickasaws and Seminoles. All of us Indians are behind you all the way. These Regulators have stolen our cattle, run roughshod through our towns and killed our people on drunken rampages. I met Colonel Copinger over at Fort Gibson and he called you Pistol Pete. Seems fitting."

"Well, I just have a score to settle and then I just want to be a cowman like you."

About that time, the lone white man, the one who had been helping with the branding, spoke up.

"Eaton, my name is Bill Knipe and I'm head of the Cattlemen's Association in Indian Territory. These folks here are my friends. I have the Bar Triangle down on the Caney River. I have a proposition for you. Might help you when you find Wyley."

"I'll need all the help I can get."

"I can make you a special officer of the Cattlemen's Association right here, right now. I'm empowered to do it. Here's your badge if you agree to wear it."

Well, I took that as a compliment for certain. I took that badge and pinned it to my shirt, and never was I prouder. If I could help out the Cattlemen's Association that would be just fine, and any help I could afford these Cherokees would make me feel some good about myself. These Cherokees were a brave people. I saw that out of Red Bird that very day when he looked down the gun barrel of a man about to murder him. Many men would have cried, screamed and begged for mercy, but Red Bird kept his composure and was ready to die with dignity. That's a rare thing.

"Do you have to swear me in or some such?"

"No sir. Just bring back news that you finished Wyley Campsey — either kill him or send him to prison — and you'll collect a reward. And, if you want, you can have a permanent job with the Cattlemen's Association. Your call."

"I'm honored and obliged."

Red Bird walked up to me and shook my hand.

"Best of luck, Frank Eaton. We'll also help by giving you about two months worth of jerked beef to take with you."

"I can use that. That way, I can spend more time concentrating on finding Wyley and dealing with him when I do."

"Will you have some beef and beans with us?"

"Let's bury these dead buzzards first."

I spent the rest of the day with my new

Cherokee friends and with my new employer, Bill Knipe. A sky tinted with orange and red slowly turned to a sky bedecked with a million stars and a bright moon. We drank coffee, ate that staple of cowboy food, beef and beans, and conversed around the campfire well into the night.

I've always been friends with them Cherokee folks and so it was good catching up with them that evening. We exchanged the news of the country thereabouts, and that meant talking about such things as events from the Chisholm Trail over to the west, all the new ranches springing up across the territory, and the likely future of it all with murdering Regulators running amok. And, when we talked of Regulators, the name of Wyley Campsey came up, as it always did when that passel of rattlesnakes was mentioned.

Folks in the Indian Territory knew about the Regulators and how they were not a bunch to trifle with, but they also knew that Wyley was in another pay grade altogether. Folks quivered at the mention of his name. He was worst of the lot. I could tell by the looks on their faces that my new Cherokee friends thought I was some loco to want to hunt that bastard down.

But, that's just what I set out to do the

following morning. It was time to see that New Mexico country. Red Bird insisted on giving me a gift of binoculars to use on my jaunt into and out of New Mexico, and I was some obliged to accept, giving him and his men a heartfelt thanks for the hospitality.

I said my adieus to my new friends and told them I would be coming back in due course to collect that reward money from the Cattlemen's Association.

I could tell by their looks that some of them Cherokee boys thought they'd never see me again.

12

It made sense at the time to head west toward the region men later called Cherokee Outlet country, staying close to the Cimarron River when possible, and making a beeline toward what is now the Oklahoma panhandle and enter New Mexico through its northeastern section. Then I would head down to Albuquerque.

The third night out on the trail I got me another of those damn premonitions, and it wasn't divining anything good. Goose pimples welled up on my arms, the hair on the back of my neck stood up and my heart went to pounding at a good clip. By this point in my life, I knew to trust those forewarnings. They always hold true. Same goes for you, son. Trust your feelings about things. If you get a bad feeling in your gut about something or somebody, then take heed. I believe the Good Lord outfits us with all kinds of natural defenses like that when we're cooking in the womb, a natural result of all of our ancestors who have lived down through the many thousands of years or longer. Their experiences carry on over to us in these days. Don't ever doubt it.

Leastways, I sat there in my campsite near the Arkansas River just contemplating things when the omen set in. I had been thinking all kinds of thoughts about Adelita, about Wyley Campsey, about what New Mexico would look like, and about those damn dreams that haunted me of a night. I couldn't quite put a finger on the omen's full meaning on that first night, but I was some certain that it had to do with Regulators, and that I had best be watching my back trail with eagle eyes. I was already making fireless camps, and determined right then to continue the practice at least until this hunt was over.

Just to play it safe, I gathered up my gear, saddled Bo, and then lit out for another campsite a few miles distant and away from the river. I figured such decisions oftentimes make up the difference between living and dying.

Making my way across the country the next day, I made it a practice to check my back trail more often than not. I started checking it in the morning and kept it up all throughout the day.

It's mostly wide open plains in that part of the territory, with very few rises of the land on which to cast a good look across the country making up your back trail. To boot, I learned real quick that the glare of the sun during the early part of the day casts a haze upon the land making it hard to see clearly. That, coupled with the sun shining in your eyes, made it damned hard to get a clear picture of the country. Also, when using them field glasses Red Bird gave me, I made sure to point them away from the sun so no reflection could ricochet off the glasses and give away my location. All I can say is that I did the best I could.

Bo and me went along like that for a few days making good time, sometimes as much as thirty miles a day or more by my estimation. Fall was setting in and it was a great time to be alive.

Then, one day, as the sun cast a veil of haze across what is now the Oklahoma panhandle, I spotted a great mesa off on the western horizon. Turns out, it was the mesa that folks today call Black Mesa, the highest point in Oklahoma. By the time I reached Black Mesa, the sun was setting in the west and the haze of the sun had started to lift off the land all around me, including the country that made up my back trail.

I noticed right away the pinion pine trees growing in that part of the country. While there, I collected all the pinion nuts I could and saved them toward a batch of pemmican for later. Eventually, I ground up some of that Cherokee jerky into a sort of powder, mixed in some water from my canteen, and then worked in some of those pinion nuts. I figured I had made something pretty close to pemmican. Most folks like to add in meat fat, but I didn't have any to add.

Anyhow, I determined to get atop Black Mesa and take a good look back toward the east, as it just seemed like a good idea at the time, especially with the bad premonitions that had been making me feel uneasy. Well, I got up there, and being on top of that little flat-topped mountain seemed like being high up in a crow's nest in that part of the country. I sat there for the longest time taking in the scenery, nibbling on those pinion nuts and chewing on Cherokee jerky. The only thing that could've made it all taste better was a good, hot, strong cup of coffee. I knew better than to light a fire for coffee, though. That would've been a first-rate way to attract any man critter from miles around. No sir, I was some satisfied with what I had.

Now, for the longest time I looked off toward the east and didn't see hide nor hair of anything, not man nor beast. And, wouldn't you figure it, right as I was about to get up and lead Bo off somewhere and make a good night camp, I saw just the smallest dark spots moving around out there in the direction from which I had just traveled earlier that day. Let me tell you, I was some concerned. Scared is a better word. I didn't like none of it. It's one thing to be careful and always watch your back, but it's something else altogether when your diligent efforts pay off and you actually see something.

At first, I tried to tell myself that those tiny dark spots could be animals. Maybe it was a band of wild horses, perhaps a passel of antelope. Soon, there was damned sight more of those black spots out there, maybe fifty or more, and those spots kept getting bigger. That gave me to know that those black spots were heading right toward me. Let me tell you, my heart went to pounding and the hair on the back of my neck stood up, but not because of any premonition, but because of what was going on right before my very eyes. A minute or so later, those strange objects were more than just dark spots on the eastern horizon. They were bonafide mounted horsemen, and they were right on my trail like a bloodhound after a coon.

My ass was in a sling and I knew it, because those riders were, no doubt, that small army of Regulators Doyle Campsey had warned me about. Turns out, that sonsabitch wasn't bluffing about the size of his band of cow flies. I cursed myself a fool for doubting him and for getting myself into such a fix as this.

Son, I'm not going to lie to you none at all. Right then, I was scared out of my wits. Any man in his right mind would've been. It's one thing to have one or two men on your trail aiming to place you on the other side with all the other dearly departed. It's another thing altogether to have fifty or more chasing you down.

The tables had turned. I had gone from being the hunter to being the hunted, and the odds weren't looking none too good for me. The more I thought about it, the more it gave me an almost sickly feeling in my craw. I didn't like it.

Times like that, a man can go to questioning why he had let himself get into such a dangerous predicament. All kinds of backtracking questions ran through my mind at the time. I asked myself why I hadn't listened to Adelita and run away with her to live the free life of the gypsy. I asked myself why I hadn't found a job with one of them Texas outfits pushing longhorns up the trail to Kansas. Them outfits would be finishing up with their drives about now and them cowboys would be loaded with spending money in a wild cow town somewhere. I asked myself why I hadn't just stayed back there in the Cooweescoowee District of the Cherokee Nation and help my stepfather work his spread. I thought of mother and remembered the many times she begged me to set aside my idea of reckoning with them Regulators and let God dish up the justice. But her words were of no use. I had spent an entire boyhood preparing to even things up in that regard and told her so. I thought about the many times she heard such words from me and fought back the tears. Out there in the middle of no man's land facing a humungous band of murdering Regulators hot on my scent, I saw mother's sweet face again and again and pondered the love and wisdom behind her beautiful blue eyes.

And then I looked off to the east and spied that army of rattlesnakes and realized it was too damned late to change anything now. Like as not, a man has to live in the present. Same with me.

Even though it was close on to full darkness, I figured to keep moving along to the westward in order to put distance between me and that pack of Regulators. I walked over to Bo and told him the bad news. I knew he wanted me to take that saddle off him and rub him down for the night. I explained that I would get us out of this fix somehow and to just bear with me for now. Right as I climbed aboard Bo I saw that look in his eyes, a look that said he was some disappointed he had to keep on carrying me without a good night's rest first. I've never liked treating my animals that way.

We rested very little for the next several days as we pushed hard into New Mexico country. We found ourselves in the region of Capulin Mountain and, once I spied it to the west, I made a beeline toward that lone peak in good time. I wanted to climb the east slope of the mountain and look at my back trail.

Leaving Bo at the foot of that old volcano — for that is what Mount Capulin is, even though I didn't know it at the time — I climbed a good ways up and took a good look to the east as the sun's haze had left the country thereabouts. I always waited until the sun was behind me to the west before using those fancy binoculars Red Bird gave me. The last thing I needed was for the sun's reflection to bounce off that binocular glass and give my position away.

My heart sunk as I saw that same bunch of riders ever pushing in my direction. Them sonsabitches must've really hated my guts, I thought at the time, for they had no let up in them. So, I scooted down that slope toward Bo just as fast as I could without tumbling heels over head. At that point, I was some vexed about what my plan should be. I knew I needed to make tracks, muy pronto, but I also knew I couldn't run poor Bo to death while doing it.

To boot, it aggravated me to think about them Regulators whose horses never seem to tire. Them sonsabitches just kept pushing! I also figured they had a couple of good trackers in their party. Quality trackers were in good abundance in those years immediately after the War Between the States, because it was during that fracas that good tracking men developed their skills. It occurred to me that I had been easy prey so far on my trek to New Mexico. Lack of rain had been part of the problem. One good thunderstorm would destroy some of Bo's tracks and help keep the dust down as we traveled. But there had been no rain at all.

We pushed on.

A couple of days later, we arrived at a little mesa without too many trees and no brush covering it. After climbing to the top, I looked back over the country to the east again. Yep, my pursuers were still out there, and there was no stop in them.

I did the same thing when I got to another mesa some miles distant. There were trees that covered the bottom part of this little mesa out there in eastern New Mexico, but it's bare of anything at the top. I hiked half way up the slope, rested against a tree and surveyed my back trail, always making sure to avoid any reflection from the sun bouncing off the lenses of those binoculars. Sure enough, they were gaining on me. I had no time to tarry. Just as I began to push off and begin my descent down the slope, I heard the thud sound of lead blasting a hole in the very tree I had just leaned against.

Son, right then I knew that if I hadn't been in trouble before, I sure was deep in it now. Someone in that bunch was a helluva marksman, and they were surely packing a buffalo rifle, probably one of them 1874 Sharps. To make matters worse, that sonsabitch was close enough to draw a bead on me, and the knowledge of that had my heart pounding like a war drum.

I scurried down that slope as fast as I could with falling forward, thinking all the way about what to do next. By the time I reached Bo down at the bottom, I had made up my mind to change direction. So far, I had been traveling at a direction almost straight west, with the aim of hitting the mountain route of the Santa Fe Trail and then following along its trace southwest into the heart of that Sangre de Cristo mountain country. There, I would catch the Old Spanish Trail and make my way to Albuquerque. Right then, though, I decided to change to a more southwesterly course and, hopefully, get myself into some country that offered a little more cover. So far, I thought to myself at the time, I had been out there in open country and was making myself nothing more than a good target. I had gotten to a point where reaching Albuquerque and Wyley Campsey had taken a back seat to the notion of simply staying alive.

As much as I hated to do it, I pushed Bo into a more southwesterly course, and pushed him hard. While that didn't set well with me, I figured I had to. Almost two days of riding took us into a country dotted with mesas everywhere. Bo was one of the toughest horses I had ever owned, but I knew he was getting close to be played out, and I just wasn't going to get much more out of him, and it gave me a no account feeling in my gut to know I had run him as hard as I had up until then.

I gotta tell you, we had placed ourselves into some of the damndest looking country I had ever seen, what with all them mesas lining the horizon in every direction. Something about it gave me a good feeling.

I started scaling some of them mesas to get a feel for the country thereabouts. Right off, I noticed that most of them mesas had slopes so steep that it was some difficult for a horse to make it to the top with a man on his back. Most of the time, I had to step down off Bo and lead him upward, and often it was still a difficult climb for him. The climbs were sometimes difficult for me, too. Keeping good footing amidst a lot of loose rocks was the trick to not falling backwards down the slope.

It was my good fortune that I did not see any sign of them Regulators again for about three days after reaching that mesa country. By then, I had spent a little time scouting around the country thereabouts and getting use to it. Bo and me had left tracks everywhere, and the only thing that might have camouflaged them was a good dust storm that blew like hell for several hours on the second day.

Bo and me, we found us a pretty good mesa to hide on. It was right out there in the middle of all them other mesas, surrounded by other flat-topped mountains on all sides for miles around. There was only one trail up to the top of this mesa, and it was a tricky one to navigate while astraddle a horse. Even though I chose to lead Bo up to the top, I could've rode him up, albeit with some considerable effort to keep us both from tumbling backwards down to the base.

The beautiful thing is there was only one pathway up to our mesa-top. It began on the south side amidst a clump of small pinions and you had to be looking for it to find it. Even at the very beginning of the trail, it was rough going for man and horse and, as I said before, a man had to decide for himself whether to stay aboard his mount or lead it to the top. On that first trek up the trail, I got about half way up the mesa's slope, emerged through a narrow passageway made by boulders and thick oak brush and then turned to look back down. It was an interesting sight. I had just come through a trail that was narrow where those boulders and trees stood bunched together, but a trail that widened as I went up. At the time, I thought that part of the trail above the narrow valve resembled a lady's hand fan, and that narrow opening was the handle. Where I stood looking down was about half way up where the fan widened out. This was something I found considerably interesting, and I sort of cataloged it away in the back of my mind.

This mesa-top perch allowed me a bird's eye view for miles all around. I tied Bo off back toward the center of the mesa top where he could munch grass in behind some pinion trees, hidden-like. I crawled up in amongst some rocks and brush on the east side of the mesa and kept an almost constant look out. It was a great view off to the east and I was some confident that I was completely hidden.

I layed up there and rested, chewed on that mix of jerky and pinion nuts, and kept perfectly still. It also gave me a good feeling to know that Bo was resting, too, and munching away on grass. He would have his legs back in short order, I thought.

On the second day, as I looked off to the southwest from my hidden perch, I saw a great cloud of dust. I kept my eyes on the spectacle with some interest, as my Regulator friends would surely not be coming at me from that direction. No sir, they would be coming in from the east or northeast, and I had been watching that part of the horizon for some time and had seen nothing. I layed there for the longest time taking in the sight, and soon I was able to make out just what it was stirring up all that New Mexico dirt. It was a herd of wild horses and they had run all the way up to the same group of mesas where I lay hidden. Soon enough, the herd came into view. Leading the bunch was a powerfully built black and white stallion. He has himself a harem of mares what followed right behind him. Right about then, I heard Bo stirring in the trees not too far behind me. He heard the thundering hooves and whinnying cries of his own kind and he began neighing, snorting and whinnying himself, all the while pulling at his tether rope. It made my heart feel good knowing Bo still held the spirit of his breed deep inside, and the occasion gave me pause as I thought about how all we living creatures were created to run wild and free, and not beholden to those things that tie us down, things like the love of money and power.

I'll tell you something else about those wild mustangs what made my heart smile — them horses was destroying a lot of the tracks Bo had made as we came into that country. Them horses was making the job of them Regulator trackers all the harder and that meant I was that much safer up there in my mesa-top perch.

While I was some relieved that those horses didn't belong to my pursuers, I was also certain them Regulators would come calling in short order.

That time came in dramatic fashion on the third day when the sun was about three hours from setting behind the western horizon. As I gazed off to the southeast from my flat top mountain, one hell of an event unfolded out there in that great wide open, mesa dotted world that had become my theater.

A passel of horsemen I knew to be the Regulators were working their way around the north end of a large anvil-shaped mesa, and their general direction seemed to be toward the northwest. Looking at them horsemen through my field glasses, I saw Doyle Campsey out in front, and it almost seemed like he was looking right back up at me for a moment there. But I was some confident in my hidden crow's nest atop that mesa.

Coming around on the west side of the same mesa, out of view of them Regulators, rode what looked like an injured Comanche warrior slouched over the neck of a black mustang making its way north.

It appeared the black was ambling along of its own volition, as the Comanche appeared played out, close to death-like.

As I sat up there on my mesa-top lookout, I knew that Comanche was about to ride square into the midst of all them Regulators. At the time, I wished like hell that I could've warned that Indian to turn his mount around and ride out of that country, muy pronto, but there was no way I could've done that from my position.

Sure, I had heard aplenty of Comanche atrocities against white settlers over the years, and some of the hellish details of those cruelties could make a grown man's stomach turn, but I just didn't like what I was seeing unfold there. It surely looked like one played out Indian was about to come face-to-face with a small army of no-account murdering rattlesnakes, and it has always been a weakness of mine to see things through the eyes of the underdog, and that's exactly what that Comanche was right then and there.

In a matter of minutes, that Comanche's horse ambled around that mesa on the north side and, just that fast, them Regulators had that lone Indian covered with rifle and pistol in one of the damndest things I had ever seen during my days on the frontier. They had him dead to rights.

Of course, that Comanche wasn't slouched forward over his horse's neck any longer. He had come alive once he realized his predicament. He didn't try to evade them Regulators none at all. He was spent, as was his horse, so he just sat there and looked square in the faces of those white gunmen who had him covered real thorough-like.

I could see that words were being exchanged and figured neither party was understanding the other. That Comanche went from being limp across his horse to being extra expressive-like with his hands and arms, desperately trying to break through the language chasm with his hand signs and such. Even though that Indian was probably party to no telling what kind of savage atrocities against folks pushing westward back in those days — and I had heard those terrible stories aplenty — I still felt a certain pity for him as he faced those snakes all alone like that. Of course, that warrior was a true fighting man and the last human being on earth who wanted pity from anyone.

As I watched that scene play out through

my field glasses, I saw a Comanche warrior accepting of his fate and completely unafraid to die. I knew that I was witnessing the end of an era on the frontier, the end of a way of life of a great fighting race, and it was a sad sight.

Just as that group of six Regulators riddled father full of holes many years earlier, so did that small army of Regulators do the same to that lone Indian out there in that lonesome mesa country as I watched from my high-up perch.

Them Regulators dropped the warrior off his horse with a cowardly cascade of rifle and pistol fire, and the sight of it damn near made me sick. What a bunch of craven sonsabitches, I thought.

A group of about ten Regulators rode up around the body to survey the victim of their gutless work. After a few moments, they rode off to the west. And I knew that when they rode off they had me in mind as the next rag doll to pepper full of holes.

Once the band of horsemen had disappeared off on the western horizon, I surveyed the sun hanging above their dust and surmised that there was about two hours of daylight left, maybe a little more when considering the light you have remaining after the sun drops and completely disappears. Once I was certain them Regulators were gone for the night, I determined to perambulate down to that dead Comanche and look things over. I left Bo up on the mesa and took off by myself. I was beginning to gather that it was some difficult navigating that mesa country whilst atop a horse. Most often, them mesa slopes were too steep for horses to climb and descend, and I figured I could move about faster, quieter, and make less of a target whilst afoot, whether I was going up or down a mesa or just traversing the flat lands in between them.

As I descended the mesa slope to the flatlands below, I slid down rockslides and around loose rocks and boulders. Once down to the flats, I ran toward that dead Comanche at a good clip, stopping every now and again to survey the country all around me to make sure I was alone. It weren't my intent to meet the same end as the Comanche.

The scene of that Comanche's murder was a dastardly and grisly sight, and once I had made my way to it an unusual feeling came over me, a suspicion of being watched by something or someone.

The warrior's mustang stayed by him through it all. When I arrived at the site, the horse was munching on grass and swatting at flies with his tail. There was no saddle on the horse, as was Comanche custom. Them Comanches rode a horse just as good, if not better, than any white man, and they did so without a saddle of any kind. A sturdy leather strip had been tied around the horse's neck and that had served as reins. That stallion was no looker by back east standards, but out there in that mesa country of New Mexico as the sun began to drop, he looked like something special. That Indian had made a tough horse out of him, as he was nothing but muscle from head to tail, and the look in his eyes spoke of long raids without rest, food and water. That horse had toughness written all over him.

The leather cord around the horse's neck I appropriated for myself, tying the strip around my waist. A man can never have enough good leather when traipsing around the country alone, and I figured I could use it for tying stuff to my saddle and other assorted purposes.

I stepped over to the bullet-ridden body of the Comanche. His bloody corpse was a horrible, gruesome thing to behold, and it reminded me of what father looked like after the same was done to him back when I was a kid of a boy.

I began appraising the area where the Comanche had fallen and immediately noticed the war club hanging from the right side of the warrior's waist, a large leather sheath hanging from his opposite side, and a pair of fine-looking knee-high leather moccasins on his feet. The war club consisted of a round, fist-sized stone affixed at the end of a long wooden handle. A large swath of leather tightly covered the stone and helped keep it attached to the handle. Later on, I learned them Comanche used wet leather to tie off those stones. They drew the leather around the rock as tightly as they could and, during the drying, it contracted even tighter around the stone, holding the business end of the club firmly in place. The leather around the stone served two purposes. It not only held the rock in place, it also muffed the sound when they used it to clobber someone across the skull. Keeping things quiet might make all the difference in carrying out a successful raid. The war club was hanging from the warrior's waist and I appropriated it at once. I figured I might somehow have good use for it.

I appraised the face of the warrior and, as strange as it might seem, sympathized with his plight and that of his people. I took to talking to him as if he were alive.

"I know you're past caring, but I don't care too much for the way you were gunned down by that bunch."

The whole scene gave me to feel like something was stirring about, like something or someone was watching me. I paused for a spell to listen to the nearby sounds, to maybe catch the suspicious scent of something on the wind, but I came up with nothing but just an uneasy feeling. I reminded myself that I often got those feelings right as the sun was beginning its drop at the end of the day. It had been that way for me for many years, and for what reason I knew not.

Maybe what I felt nearby was not living, breathing humans. Maybe my senses picked up on the Great Spirit coming to collect one of his fallen warriors. Maybe the Great Spirit didn't come alone to do such work. Maybe some of those Comanches who went before came with the Great Spirit to help him collect one of their very own fighting men and take him home to beyond the veil. Maybe our senses pick up on not only the living but also those who have gone to the other side. Maybe the line between us and those beyond the veil is not a thick brick wall but a strand of chicken wire, I thought at the time and sometimes still do.

Leastways, it wasn't those on the other side causing me any shivers that evening. No siree. I was some concerned about coming up on some of those still living on this side of the line, those with weapons looking for the good kill.

I stood frozen there for a spell before feeling comfortable enough to resume my talk with that Comanche.

"I've heard of you Comanches. Heard you count many white men among your trophies. White women and children, too. Could be you deserved killing. I don't know. Leastways, I don't hold with what just happened to you."

I knelt down and untied them handsome moccasins, pulled them off his feet, inspected them more closely and determined they were not only sturdy looking but also about my size. Liking the look of them pliable Indian shoes, I rolled them up, tied them in a bundle and then latched them to my belt for carrying.

"You know, I can't figure how a Comanche warrior like you — sick and spent or not — allowed himself to stumble across those killing vermin unawares like that. Damndest thing I've ever seen with my own eyes."

Right about then, I untied the leather

sheath and reached inside for its contents. I'll be damned if he wasn't using that leather to tote the biggest and most beautiful Bowie knife I had ever seen. Figured he must have taken it off someone, one time or another. Leastways, I appropriated that, too.

"I'm taking your moccasins, war club and knife. I know you wouldn't want any of this stuff going to waste. I'm obliged to you."

As I looked at the bronze face of that Comanche, I thought of how we all have to play the cards dealt to us in this life. I figured he played his cards the way he thought best, just as I was playing mine. On another day and in another place, the two of us would probably have been enemies, but as I looked down on him on the day of his death, I found no reason to wish him anything but the best beyond the veil, and I told him so.

"I wish you the best. I don't know if your people hold with burying the dead, but I figure you don't want the coyotes ripping your body apart and the buzzards picking at your eyeballs, so I'm burying you here beneath this here mesa as best I can."

I found a patch of nearby brush where the ground underneath seemed softer than in most other spots near the area. I found a flat stone and dug out a hole as best I could.

The hole wasn't near six-feet deep, that much I can tell you, but it was deep enough to hold his body. I placed him within, covered him with dirt and then placed rocks on top of that. I drew a few steps back, surveyed what I had done, and was some pleased with my work.

I looked around for that Comanche steed but he had ambled off. Now, he was on his own. The Comanche were a tough and fierce tribe of hardened warriors, and they expected the same steel from their horses. I had heard them warriors would ride the hell out of a horse in such a way that either killed it or made it one robust mount. I figured the horse that had belonged to the Comanche I just buried was an example of that sturdy breed.

With only a few minutes to go until the dark of night set in, I gathered up my belongings and started walking back toward my mesa. Right as I brushed past a boulder at the bottom of the mesa near the burial site, a bullet whizzed by my head and ricocheted off a boulder at the mesa base. That was the second time them sonsabitches tried to assassinate me from a distance and I was starting to get damned tired of it.

Them Regulators must have left someone behind to scout the area whilst the main party looked off to the westward, I figured at the time. But I didn't know for sure. And, by then, the night was dark enough to keep an assassin from even knowing for sure that it was me they were aiming at. He could've been aiming at what he thought was a Comanche coming to find their injured warrior. Leastways, I didn't wait around to find the answers to any of these questions. I skedaddled out of there at a good clip heading in the opposite direction of my home mesa. I wasn't about to lead anyone there. A few minutes rolled by before the world was dark all around. Once I was sure the black of night shrouded me in its midst, I turned myself back around and made for my mesa-top perch, running quickly and quietly.

Then I went to thinking about that assassin back there by where I buried the Comanche. If the gunman, or *gunmen,* them Regulators left behind figured it was me they were shooting at then they would surely have the main body alerted to my whereabouts, and muy pronto. This time the next day, I surmised, this area would be crawling with Regulators.

When I got back to my mesa, I looked off to the west and spotted a campfire many miles distant. I knew that fire represented the camp of the Regulators that had taken off to the west after murdering that Comanche.

The next day proved me right. It was still morning when I gazed down onto the flats and saw the country all around crawling with Regulators, and the sight of it made me feel some uneasy in my gut. They were down there amidst them mesas broke up in small groups looking for yours truly and some of them were edging mighty close to my mesa. I figured most men would look at the slopes of my little flat-topped mountain and deem them too steep for man and horse to climb. And they would be mostly right — that is, unless they found my trail to the top, and they damned near had to be looking for that pathway in order to find it. And there was another thought of mine that made me feel a little more confident about my hidden roost. The hired gunmen that made up the Regulators' ranks didn't look like the type of fellows what wanted to get down off their horses and do any real work — work like leading horses up a rocky, steep mesa slope that could give way under man and horse and send them all downward topsy-turvy into a pile at the bottom. No sir, they saw themselves as paid killers first, horsemen second, and trying to pry them off their mounts would be nigh impossible.

I watched the goings-on for a couple of hours before the entire band got together and pow-wowed in a big meeting-like. That's when they began heading off toward the southern horizon and to the mesas down that way. They seemed to have given up finding me in the area where I lay hidden. Whilst that knowledge made me feel some better, I also knew they wouldn't give up their search until they had me cornered for the good kill. The thought of it was almost too much for my gut to abide.

There I was in one fine situation, a predicament of my very own making. Because I was so hell-bent on settling the score with father's murderers, and had balanced with all but one to finish the job, I had put myself up against an army of killers knocking on my door out there in the middle of New Mexico mesa country. I just hadn't planned for anything like this. Taking care of Doc, Shannon, Jim and Jonce had been nothing compared to what I now faced. That's because I had lived and practiced for that kind of work for years on end, steady-like. I had never envisioned facing a small army.

I just couldn't believe it had all come to this. I thought of all the folks in settled towns everywhere living in nice houses, sleeping in soft beds of a night, and enjoying paid lawmen to help keep order. And I compared that to the damned living nightmare playing out before my very eyes. I thought of how they had gunned down father and how they had tortured and killed Marshal Adams. As I sat up there on my mesa looking at the dust made by that passel of gunmen, scouring the country for my skin, I thought of how I might very well end up joining father and Chris on the other side of the veil right soon.

To be honest, I was feeling some sorry for myself. I spent the whole day down in the doldrums and thinking about how them Regulators would never give up until I was dead.

Night came and it weren't too many hours before a small speck of light appeared on the southern horizon. I knew that light represented a Regulator campfire many miles distant. Right about then, a west wind blew in that gave me to pause. It was a fierce blow, and I took off my hat to let the wind that cooled my face also blow through my now long hair. I drank in the cool breeze, letting it cool not only my body but also the scorching hot thoughts I had lived with all that day. I looked off at that far away campfire, felt the night wind drench my body and soul in its coolness, and the whole scene sent my brain into a flurry of thought.

And that's how I fell asleep that night, just pondering that far-off campfire and the men who sat and slept around it.

The next day I arose feeling some better about this old world and my place in it. I had done a heap of thinking and a game plan was slowly but surely forming for me to follow. The whole idea had come down on me from the night wind, sort of like the epiphanies them Bible men talk about.

Later that afternoon, as I sat up there on my mesa pondering what to do about them Regulators, that same herd of wild mustangs came helling in from out of the north. At first, I heard their thundering hooves pound against the flat lands. I caught sight of them and it was apparent they were making their way back to the vicinity of my mesa. Bo heard them, too. He went to snorting and stomping and whinnying and generally making a damned spectacle of himself.

It was natural, I thought, that the call of his own kind pulled at him just as the moon pulls the sea waters that makes for the high tide. It was right then that another of them epiphanies hit me. And I acted on it, muy pronto.

I grabbed up Bo and ran my hands down

along his head, neck and withers. I rubbed my face up against his face and patted him in thanks and appreciation for all the good rides he had given me, jaunts with an old friend that I would never forget. And I told him so.

"Bo, I'm going to miss you, my friend. Thanks for everything."

Of course, Bo had kept up with the neighs and the whinnies, the snorting and the stomping, and I didn't want to hold him back any longer.

"Bo, you know I'm better off afoot in this country up against that passel of snakes down there. I gotta be able to travel quiet-like and unseen. I gotta be able to strike fast and oily-like. I just can't risk Doyle Campsey and that bunch hearing you whinny or seeing your dust."

I put them reins back on him and commenced to leading him across the mesa-top and over to the trail. I led him down to the bottom real careful-like. I gave him one last rub on the neck and whispered into his ear that I would surely miss him. Then I removed those reins and slapped him on his rump. By then, those mustangs had made some tracks, but were still visible heading off toward the southwest. Bo lit out to join them like his tail was on fire, and it made my heart sing to see a creature running off to be free with his own kind. We men can only wish to be as free as that, but it's a dream we'll never realize. No sir, just as soon as we men are born we inherit the problems and conditions of the world into which we have been placed, and there's no getting around it. We have to rise to the occasion and face up to the challenges like men. You know, I had never asked for them six murderers to ride up and kill father that night, and I had never asked that father get himself crosswise with them bastards by engaging in his Vigilante activities in the first place. But, the fact is them sonsabitches killed my father in cold blood, and I had made a vow to even it all up. But even without making such a vow, I had it in my craw to do it. And so there I was, living out a life that had sort of been set up for me to play out as needs must.

I watched Bo until he disappeared beyond the horizon, removed my hat and bade him one last farewell.

Many would surely ask why I would intentionally place myself afoot out in the middle of mesa country whilst a gang of the worst kind of cutthroats rode the trail for my ass. The answer was that, by that time, I had determined a course of action that made riding a horse obsolete. Bo had been kicking up dust, leaving tracks and generally making our whereabouts known to those Regulator trackers. From then on, I knew I had to move about like a ghost, quiet-like and making no tracks.

Sometimes a man just gets a gut full. I had taken all I was going to take from them bastards out there. Here I was in new country running around like a scared cur from them sonsabitches what had mowed down father, tortured and killed Chris Adams and shot that spent Comanche right off his horse for no good reason. I was done running. If those craven cowards wanted some of me then they were about to get it — on my terms. I thought of all the running from them I had done in recent days and I grew angry with myself and cursed myself for a cowardly sister boy. No more. At that point, I didn't care a damn if I ended up blown full of holes and sent to the world beyond the veil.

I went back up to my mesa-top and watched the darkness of night spread its fingers around the country thereabouts. I kept my eyes pointed off to the south hoping to catch sight of another Regulator campfire. It weren't too long before I detected the far distant twinkle of just such a thing. The position of that campfire out there on the southern horizon gave me to know them Regulators had moved further south and west in their search for me. It made my heart happy that I had dodged them so far and that they were unaware of my location, and that they were drifting further away from me in their search. That made me to feel some confident in my mesa-top hideout.

I pulled off them boots of mine and tossed them into the brush. I grabbed up them knee-high Comanche moccasins and slid them on my feet, raising the tops up to right below my knees and securing them with a leather cords around my legs. Them moccasins fit just fine! I sure liked the feel of that soft leather around my feet and legs. Once I started walking around in them Indian shoes, I realized just how much them boots of mine had kept me all bound up. My feet and legs were used to carrying around them heavy boots, so when I stood up in those moccasins and walked around a little, I felt like I could run a hundred miles and jump around like an antelope.

Then I grabbed up that Comanche war club, held it in my hands for a bit just to get the feel of it, and then tied it to my belt. I liked the way that club felt in my hands.

Some Comanche, probably the one I buried, made that weapon to have near perfect balance.

On my opposite waist, tied to my belt, I also carried that Bowie knife inside of its thick leather sheath. I was packing a lot of weaponry when you figure I still sported both of my sidearms.

From out of my canteen, I poured a little water onto a patch of dirt, mixed the dirt and water around real good with my fingers until I had some nice, thick mud. Then, I applied hefty amounts of that mud all over my face, covering my forehead and cheeks real thorough-like.

Then I stood up on that mesa and looked once more toward that far-off campfire, sort of calculating in my mind the best route to get there as I skirted between all the mesas along the way. I figured that Regulator camp was about ten miles south of my mesa. I knew beyond a shadow of a doubt that camp was where I wanted to be so I took off at once.

I went to the trail and commenced walking carefully down the rocky trail to the mesa's base. From down below, I could no longer see the distant campfire, blocked as it was by all those mesas in between it and me. But I had studied the layout of the land from up on my mesa well enough that I had a good idea how to get there, muy pronto.

My next stop was a certain Regulator camp for a surprise social call.

13

The cool fall wind felt mighty good against my mud-caked face as I made my way toward the light of the Regulator campfire. I jogged a good part of the distance and never even broke a sweat. In fact, that cool night air just hardened that mud glaze to my face and that made me feel some better about my camouflage.

The closer I got to the area of the campfire the more I slowed my pace. Eventually, my pace decreased to a good gait and then a steady, careful walk. The last thing I wanted was to run hell for breakfast into a sentry watching the outer parameters of the camp. No sir, that would have ruined all my plans.

About five hundred yards out from the fire I stopped to just look and listen, taking things in a sort of calculating way, slow-like. I figured this excursion needed to be free of mistakes, so I kept a wary demeanor, constantly telling myself there was no need to hurry because I had all night to carry out my plans for them Regulators.

At that distance, I could tell their camp was nestled amidst a good crop of trees at the base of a mesa. I commenced crawling down low the rest of the way in. Now, I gotta tell you, trying to tote that rifle while crawling was sort of tricky business. I tried to keep the rifle barrel from scraping or nicking stones as I inched along. A few times, the rifle barrel struck a rock in my path and the sound of it hit my ears like the boom of a cannon, and I froze with fear each time, fearful as I was of making even the slightest noise and giving myself away. The metal framing my pistol grips was also of some concern as I crawled along, but not as much as the rifle barrel. I cleared out any objects in my pathway as I went, which made for less noise as the rest of my body came along after, if you know what I mean. That war club was perfect for slithering around low to the ground easy and quiet-like. The business end of the club was covered real good in leather and made no sound when it hit objects, and the wooden handle offered much the same benefit. The Bowie I carried in the same leather sheath I found it in, so it didn't worry me none as a noisemaker.

My belt buckle was another matter altogether. It scraped rocks a few times and I allowed for that as I inched along. Had I thought about it more carefully beforehand, I would have figured out a way to cover that buckle in leather before setting out on this middle of the night jaunt. Since I was using my belt to carry my holstered pistols and sheathed knife, I just had to allow that belt and its buckle as necessary to the night's work ahead. Again, I tried to do a good job of clearing stones from my pathway with my hands as I crept along so the buckle wouldn't have anything to nick.

Making my way to about fifty yards out from the fire took several hours, careful as I was to make myself an unseen, unheard ghost in the darkness. I crawled to an area of cottonwoods and rocks large enough to hide behind, stood up and looked again toward the fire. Being up that close gave me a good view of the goings-on in the encampment. Several men sat near the fire. Looked like they were drinking coffee. Every now and again, someone would emerge from the darkness around the fire and into my view.

A familiar looking fellow eventually walked out and sat by the fire, and it didn't take too long for me to see it was Doyle Campsey. He was facing directly out in my direction, and there were times when it seemed he was looking directly at yours truly, right into my eyes. He poured a cup of coffee, clutched it in his hands, and then stood up all to once and cupped his hands around his right ear like he had heard something unusual or unexpected from outside the camp.

The sight of that made me feel some alarmed. The last thing I needed was Regulators scouring the country hereabouts looking in my direction. I immediately moved back behind that big cottonwood and kept perfectly still, listening to my heart pound. A few moments passed and I peered back their way again. A group of about five men gathered around Doyle and they all powwowed together for a time.

They must have decided that whatever Doyle thought he had heard was nothing after all, because the whole bunch sat back down and commenced drinking coffee and talking. That Regulator camp went right back to acting normal and that was just fine with me.

I stood there against that cottonwood for a spell and decided them Regulators had calmed down enough for me to move in closer. I then crept in another twenty or thirty yards closer on a crawl, found myself another tree to crouch behind and stayed put for about an hour. Members of the encampment were still awake and talking.

Of a sudden, a fellow emerged from out of the darkness of the camp and into the firelight. He stood there for a few seconds and began making his way right in my direction. Boy, I stood as motionless as any man could and listened to my heart pound and felt the hair on the back of my neck stand up. It's funny as I think back on it after all these many, many years. The pounding of my heart I could hear in my head, and the sound was so loud to me that I figured the whole world could hear it, too. That's how the mind sometimes works in situations such as that. The exhilaration of the moment mixed in with a healthy dose of fear keeps the senses on high alert and gives the mind all kinds of silly things to worry on. I just kept telling myself to play it cool, calm and quiet.

There's something else I think about those days. I'm an old man now, and nigh to visiting all those others beyond the veil, but I was cold and calculating in those days long ago. It makes my heart shudder now to revisit those times and ponder how I stood there cold and quiet waiting to pounce on those demon bastards in the middle of the night the way I did. I think about how stone cold crazy I was to embark on such a job. I saw what they did to father, to Chris Adams and to that Comanche. They would do the same or worse to me. I'd stung them good and they were poison mad at the sound of my name. It was damned dangerous business.

I stood there as still as a rock with big eyes peering through a camouflaged face, keeping my breathing steady and thinking how easy it would be to sneeze or cough and send the whole scene into a bullet-flying frenzy.

Of a sudden, a Regulator walked out of the darkness to a large clump of sagebrush and scrub oaks barely eight feet from where I stood. He just stood there for a few seconds and looked around, but I was certain that my presence was unknown to him. I quietly reached down to my belt and plucked one of them sturdy rawhide cords I had taken off that Comanche. About that time, he unbuckled his belt and began relieving himself, and I knew this because I could hear the puddling sound in the otherwise quiet of the night.

With one end of that leather cord wrapped around my left hand, and the other wrapped around my right, with about eighteen inches in between, I made one swift yet quiet move toward that Regulator, throwing that leather strip around his neck when I got there, twisting and tightening it so hard as to immediately disable him. In almost the same movement, holding that cord ever tighter around the neck, I brought him down with his back to the ground. I know my face must have been grimacing as I used every muscle in my hands and arms to squeeze the life out of that sonsabitch. Leastways, whatever struggle he might have intended to use that night, he never got a chance to utilize because I came on him quiet, quick and greasy fast, strangling him in just a matter of seconds.

I left the lifeless body where it had dropped and retreated to my spot behind the cottonwood and never took my eyes off that camp. It wasn't too very long before another Regulator ambled out of the encampment walking along the same pathway as the previous one. When he reached the vicinity of his fallen comrade, I made one quick, quiet leap and bashed his brains out with that Comanche war club. He dropped hard to the ground like a sack of potatoes. Just as before, I got back behind my cottonwood, watching, waiting.

Maybe five minutes went by and numerous figures appeared around the campfire, adding to the four or so who were already sitting there. One of them motions his hands out toward the area of my victims, and a general sense of commotion seemed to have come over the camp. I began to hear raised voices and see men walking back and forth across the campsite. I had lit the fuse and things were about to get interesting, no getting around it. One of them Regulator fellows walked out to the edge of the camp where the firelight met the darkness and called out. I'll never forget the names.

"Buck! Mont!"

Four of his friends walked up behind to join him, and then the group commenced a search for their missing companions. They walked along the same pathway as the others had, and I knew that I was about to have five Regulators right there by me and, as strange as it might sound, I welcomed the idea. Of a sudden, real convenient-like, I had five man-size shadows not more than twelve feet from me, each of them separated out real nice making nice distinct, individual targets. Just as slowly and quietly as I could — but without blowing my chance at such nice, close targets — I outs with my right-side firearm and filled the night with the thundering boom of five shots that sent five men to beyond the veil on an otherwise peaceful night in one of the most beautiful mesa-filled spots in the American West. A damned shame it was to spoil such a tranquil scene, but also damned necessary by my estimation at the time. Had I procrastinated, those men could have discovered me first and I might have been the one sent across the great divide.

I knew the time had come for me to leave the vicinity, muy pronto. But I chose not to run out of there all willy-nilly like my tail was on fire. No sir, them sonsabitches didn't know my exact whereabouts that dark night. To boot, they didn't know who had just done the shooting. As far as they knew, maybe it was one of them Regulators who stepped out of camp who did the shooting. Leastways, no one came hustling out of that camp just yet, but I knew that if I waited around long enough someone surely would. Anyway, I just walked out of there quiet and slow-like until I was maybe fifty yards out and then I commenced a very slow jog. When I was a little further out, I stopped to listen toward my back trail. Sure enough, I soon heard raised voices and that gave me to know them dead men had just been found, all seven of them. I lit out of there at a comfortable run, careful to not fall into any prairie dog holes or into trees and rocks. Of all nights to break a leg, this one wasn't it.

I got back to my mesa-top in due course and well before the sun came up the next day. That mesa-top had become my home in a sense. I felt safe there. The autumn days were getting cooler, and the nights more so. The next day after my little attack, I crawled into a hollow amidst some rocks on the southeast side of the mesa and went to sleep. The sunlight found its way to my spot and warmed me just fine. I sort of slept with one eye open if you know what I mean. My perch offered me a grand view of the vista to the south, and that's where them Regulators were still holing up, I was sure. If they somehow figured my location, which I doubted strongly they could, they would be coming at me from the south.

I would sleep some and then wake up and sort of wrestle with thoughts of them Regulators. Then I would sleep a little more and wake up to ponder them some more, and so on.

I thought a lot about Doyle Campsey and the rest of them Regulators, what they might be doing, what they might be thinking, and what they might be discussing amongst themselves. I tried to put myself into their shoes. If I were one of them, what would I be thinking after the little party I put on for them the night before?

First off, would they even believe it was me who raised all of that hell? I slithered in and out of there wearing those Comanche moccasins, so leaving no boot prints might suggest to them that their seven friends fell victim to a Comanche or two seeking revenge against them Regulators for killing one of their own. Maybe Doyle and them Regulators were wondering if some Comanches watched them from afar as they shot that warrior off his horse. To boot, when they looked at my first two kills, they would see a fellow who had been strangled and another who had been clobbered on the head. Those kind of kills might give them reason to suspect Comanche work. And, if it was their work, how many other Comanches were out there waiting to pounce on them again? The fact that this mesa land sat right in the middle of Comanche country further strengthened that line of thought. If they believed that notion, they would probably just try and fight shy of any of the tribe for fear of getting into a bigger fracas than they might want. I figured them Regulators were nothing but cowards. Sure, they would have their fun with a lone rider out in the middle of nowhere, like Chris Adams and like that Comanche, and they would surely ride up to a man's front door and shoot him full of holes as he faced them from his front porch. But them sonsabitches wanted no part of a real fight, and that's just what they would get if they tackled a passel of Comanches.

If they considered me their night raider, and not one or two Comanches seeking revenge, then they would be asking a whole lot of other questions. They would be thinking how I had seemingly fallen off the face of the earth those last few days before stinging them in the dark of the night unawares. They would be asking any manner of questions about your truly. Where had he been holed up? Why haven't we seen any of his tracks or seen any dust kicked up by his horse? Was that night raid he made on us just a stroke of luck because he accidently ambled by our camp? Or was he watching us all the time? Where in all this vast mesa country was he? Was he constantly moving around? Or did he have one favorite place to stay at? They would be asking themselves all kinds of questions and having all kinds of conversations. The more I thought about it, the more I was certain that Doyle Campsey would order his men to scour the countryside harder than ever, to go through it with a fine tooth comb until they had me cornered somewhere for first the slow torture and then the kill. He would break his men up into groups and send them out in different directions looking for me. Given enough time, they would inspect every mesa-top, every arroyo, every cottonwood-lined creek in the country until they either found me or became convinced I had vamoosed out of the country altogether.

Those were the kind of thoughts running through my mind as I lay in the sun resting the day after my night raid.

Somewhere in there, I told myself to quit thinking about their actions and to begin considering mine. To hell with what they were going to do or not do. I couldn't help any of that. What was I going to do? I commenced turning that over in my mind real earnest-like for the longest time. Yet regardless of how deep I reached into the deck, I couldn't come up with any face cards. Nothing at all came to me.

But, as the sun neared the edge of the western horizon and the country thereabouts fell under the great evening shadow, a great gust of wind blew in from the southwest and kissed my face and body. I stood up, removed my hat, and allowed the cool breeze to blow through my hair. I drank it in, relishing every moment. I stood there like that for the longest time, never thinking, just breathing and absorbing and enjoying the time and place in which I found myself, asking nothing, expecting nothing.

It was right about then that an inspiration fell over me, a revelation so obvious and real that I wondered how I hadn't thought of it before. The insight came to me unexpected and of a sudden in the form of words straight out of my own mouth as I beheld the great mesa-filled vista to the south. "What is the last thing them Regulators would expect right now?"

The answer came to me just as easy as did the great chill gusts out of the southwest. The last thing them gnarly sonsabitches would expect is another nighttime raid against them just like the one I stung them with the night before — and not tomorrow, not the next day, but tonight! That's right, two hornet stings right in a row. They would never expect that kind of audacity out of me or anyone else. They would expect last night's attacker to lay low and relive the glory over and again in his mind, to pat himself on the back. They would think the attacker would want to wait a few more days and allow them Regulators to get lazy and less watchful.

It was settled.

I determined right then and there them Regulators were going to get another social call that very night. I figured I would have the element of surprise and that gave me some confidence and motivation to get started, muy pronto. I looked up in the night sky and beheld a quarter moon and an endless sky full of stars. That was all the light I needed. I figured them Regulators were still off to the south somewhere, maybe not in the same spot, but not too many miles distant.

Just like I had the previous night, I covered my face in mud and collected all of my necessaries. I grabbed up my war club, my Bowie, my leather cords. Of course, my pistols and rifle were fully loaded. I remembered to tie a square of leather over my belt buckle to minimize any noise I might make as I crept along low to the ground in the darkness. I gave thought to covering my pistol grips in leather, but quickly abandoned that idea when I considered that covering those grips might hinder a smooth, easy grab of those weapons in a tight situation. No sir, I would just have to work hard at not letting those grips scrape any rocks as I crawled along. Those pistols had served me well up to then, and I wanted them at the ready.

When just the right amount of darkness set in for my liking, I climbed down, reached the base of the mesa and took off at a slow jog across the flatland. My goal was to keep a pace that allowed me to scan the country thereabouts as I went along in the dark. I sure didn't want to proceed along fast-like into a prairie dog hole and break my leg or into an outlying group of Regulators and get shot up.

After scooting along afoot for maybe fifteen miles to the south and eventually to the southwest, and seeing no sign of a Regulator camp, I decided to climb a nearby mesa that stood a little taller that the others in the vicinity and take me a good look around.

Now, let me tell you something. I'll never forget that second night on the prowl for them curs. A great satisfaction welled up within me as I accepted my new job as a Regulator hunter. I enjoyed it. After my success of the night before, I realized just how much excitement a man can derive from hunting down murderers in the dark of night. These sonsabitches were ruthless and smart, and working to make the good kill on them was some exhilarating. To boot, they deserved killing more than any antelope or elk.

I remember climbing the rocky slope and making my way to the mesa top. I looked out across the vastness of the night sky and felt the breeze kiss my face. I was some stricken by that never-ending dark blanket filled with those many millions of stars and that waxing quarter moon colored with just the least bit of yellow. I took all of that in and realized that I had gone from feeling like desperate prey in the face of all those Regulators to actually enjoying my new job as a Regulators hunter. I knew I was one of the luckiest men in the world to be where I was at that place and at that time with the promise of more good kills ahead of me.

I panned the area below the southern sky and looked intently for quite a spell before catching just the smallest twinkle of light maybe five miles off to the south. That was my Regulators. It looked like they had decided to keep a much smaller fire after the stinging I gave them the night before. I couldn't believe they opted to have a fire at all. I sure wouldn't have. Their fire gave me to know they didn't reckon the odds of a second straight attack were that great. That's just what I wanted them to think.

Leastways, I took a good look at that distant speck of light and sort of placed its location in my mind in relation to all the other landmarks nearby. I knew that once I got back to the flatland everything would look different.

I got down off that mesa and commenced that slow jog of mine toward the fire. It weren't no time before I was sitting behind a huge stand of sagebrush clumps and scrub oaks barely fifty feet from the fire.

I had myself a fair view of the camp, even though the area immediately around the fire lay hidden to me because that small fire just didn't give off enough light. I would just have to deal with that, I thought at the time.

Someone looking very much like Doyle Campsey sat by the fire nursing a cup of coffee, just as he was doing the night before. All around him, shadows of men went back and forth around the camp.

About that time, a fellow walks in from the darkness surrounding the camp and sits down beside Doyle. Even from the distance, and as bad as the light was, the fellow who joined Doyle looked familiar. The two started talking to beat the band. I could hear the distant murmur of their talking but couldn't make out exactly what it was they were saying. I wanted to hear them, and get a better look at the camp layout, so I decided to snake my way in closer.

After quietly slithering my way along, I was able to get to a spot within about twenty feet of the fire. I was some proud of myself for pulling that feat off without making a sound. My nest was a good little bunch of sagebrush clumps and scrub oaks near a few large rocks and an ancient cottonwood. Clouds had begun closing in and shielding the earth below of all of that moonlight, so I felt safe and sound where I lay crouched at the ready. Every time I considered the consequences of coughing or sneezing I got the jitters all over, so I tried to push those kind of thoughts out of my mind.

Of a sudden, I heard a thud-like sound off to my right. I trained my eyes on the area from where the sound came, made out some dark silhouettes and shadows, and quickly determined I was looking at the Regulator remuda. Once I was certain that passel of horses was unguarded, I trained my eyes back over to the campfire.

Like I said, that fellow sitting by Doyle looked familiar, and when I took a closer look, and did some recollecting, I knew him to be a fellow from back near home named Tom Biscane, otherwise known as Tulsa

Tom by most. He came from back in the Cherokee Nation and was known by many thereabouts, but I didn't know he ran with Regulators. I'm telling you, that Regulator network lassoed in quite a few men back in those days.

Doyle clutched his coffee cup while looking right out into the sagebrush and scrub oaks where I lay crouched. Even though I was some confident and secure in my hidden position, my heart went to beating and the hair on the back of my neck got that tickly feeling when it seemed like Doyle was looking directly into my eyes. They went to talking again and I could hear every word.

"I don't like it, Tom."

"Yeah? What is it?"

"Got a bad feeling, that's all."

"We're safe tonight. If that was Eaton — and I'm sure it was — there ain't no way in hell he's brazen enough to come back and try that stunt again, what with all the men we got."

Of a sudden, the clouds camouflaging the moon drifted off and allowed more light to hit the ground. It was right about then that my eyes made out some of the bedrolls containing men in and around the camp. I kept those spots sort of fixed in my mind.

The two Regulators went to talking again.

"Just the same, Tom, send four or five men outside the camp and look around a bit. I want no more surprises."

Well, when I heard those words my heart went to pounding, and hard. There I was twenty feet from their fire and Regulators were about to spread out from the camp and look around for yours truly. I told myself that my position was so close that none of them would think to look where I lay. As much as that reasoning had a ring of truth to it, I decided to quietly perambulate my way back out of there another forty feet or so. And I needed to do it quickly but also quietly before Tulsa Tom had time to get his men to bear for the search.

I commenced gingerly moving back in the direction from whence I came until I was about sixty feet out from the fire. About then, my eyes saw the black forms and shadows of men ambling out of the camp in all directions. One of them started from the fire and began making a slow, search-like walk straight toward me. I stood behind another one of those massive cottonwoods and didn't make a peep, watching that fellow's every move until he was about five feet away from me. He turned his back to me and looked back toward the camp. He shouldn't have done that because that's when I reached down, took hold of the war club, and then came out from behind that tree and clobbered the living daylights out of him with one savage blow.

He hit the ground and lay there in a crumple. I figured this was good work because none of it made too much of a sound. Someone close by could've heard the thud against his head and his body hit the ground, but I was some confident no one else was that close at the moment. But I also knew that men were out scouring the area around the camp and I could be joined by another visit in a heartbeat. I reached down and appropriated the sidearms off the dead body with the intention of keeping them close to hand. I had an idea I would need them.

I tucked both his guns in my belt and then also decided to take that big, fancy, wide-brimmed Regulator hat off his head. It seemed like all them Regulators wore some kind of big, fancy hat what drew attention.

Leastways, I had an idea for that hat. Being as it was the middle of the night, what I was looking for were silhouettes in the darkness, shadow figures and such-like. That's exactly what those Regulators would be looking for, too. It was too dark to look for anything else. I put on that hat and figured that it sure made me look just like one of those Regulators in all of that darkness.

About that time, I saw a black outline of a man come into my view, and he was maybe twenty-five feet from me. I figured that was as good a time as any to try my plan.

I got his attention by whispering a "psst" his direction. All to once, that Regulator came to a dead stop and began trying to decipher what the hell was going on. I placed a finger up to my lips to motion him to stay quiet. When I did that, he just nodded back in the affirmative. I then motioned to a spot to my left as if to tell him I saw something moving in that direction. Again, he nodded that he understood my meaning.

I stepped off maybe five steps toward the direction I had pointed and then turned back around to my Regulator. I pointed again in the same direction as before and nodded my head up and down, as if to say, "There's our man." The Regulator nodded back.

Then, I motioned the Regulator to step on up beside me, working my arm in a slow roll, indicating "come slowly." He made a slow walk in my direction and that's when I placed my right hand around the wood handle of that war club. I kept the leather strip attached to the wood handle tied in a sort of slipknot around my belt, so it weren't no problem bringing that weapon to bear with one hand.

Right as he got in striking distance he sort of hesitated a bit and that gave me to know that maybe he had realized his mistake at the last minute. I didn't want him to holler for his friends so in one, slick, oily-like motion I brought that club up and cracked his skull immediately. If the initial blow didn't kill him right off, he didn't last too much longer after he hit the ground. When I reached down to appropriate his sidearms his was a completely limp and lifeless body. That Comanche war club was one well-built and effective weapon that downed men for good and did it on the quiet.

I appropriated both his pistols at once, tucking them behind my belt. Right about then, I looked back toward the fire and saw the dark outlines of six men barely forty feet from me, and they looked to be slowly making their way in my direction. They weren't acting in any way like they had heard what had just happened with their now dead friend. They were just sort of casually searching in the darkness.

That was the moment when I determined Frank Eaton had just about milked all the action out of this excursion that he could. I decided to end the night with a flair and then saunter on out of there, muy pronto. I ups with one of my very own sidearms, because I knew it was fully loaded, and then fired a lightening quick cascade of rounds into those six men, dropping each of them where they had stood. The boom of gunfire filled the night and I knew that would be the spark to set off the powder keg. I looked back over toward the camp and saw a passel of about fifteen Regulators assembled around the fire looking off in my direction trying to determine just what the hell had happened. Some of them began calling for their friends to return to camp.

I quickly re-holstered my sidearm. Then, using the pistols appropriated from my first kill that night, fired into the camp and downed as many of them sonsabitches as I could. I calculated that I had shot up just about every one of those standing by the fire. After that, I raised my rifle and sprayed all of that area where I had noticed the bedrolls earlier. I heard the screams and cries of multiple men and that gave me to know I had done some good. I figured I ventilated at least twenty-five men that night, maybe more.

I dropped all of those Regulator sidearms on the ground, keeping only my very own weapons, and then began ambling back out of there.

I quickly yet quietly disappeared into the deep darkness more than a hundred yards out from the camp, stopped for a moment to listen to any sounds, heard nothing unusual, and then proceeded back to my mesa.

14

I woke the next morning some proud of my previous night's work. As I lay there in my sleeping spot on the southeast side of the mesa, chewing on my very own version of pemmican and letting the sun warm my body, I thought of my next move. I never did have an exact count of them Regulators what had followed me out to that mesa country, but I had always figured their number to about fifty-five or sixty men. By my best calculations, I surmised that I had killed maybe half of them, perhaps wounding a few more. Leastways, I was some confident I had reduced their count by a hefty measure.

But I also knew those remaining Regulators were still out there, more cold and deadly than they had ever been, searching for me in that country off to my south. For some reason, they believed I lay holed up out that way, for that was where they had concentrated their search for me over the last several days. They just couldn't figure why they hadn't seen any of Bo's tracks. I had just dropped off the face of the earth as far as they knew.

There were two things that I was sure of as I lay there on my mesa-top perch. First, I wasn't leaving this country until I had broken up that band of gut robbers for good. Secondly, I was some sure that I couldn't go back for any more nighttime ambushes again. I had done played that option out. Now them Regulators would have men on watch all the time, and to risk another such waylay could get me killed.

A picture of that little trail up to my mesa top kept reappearing in my mind's eye. As I told you before, a little ways up that trail, the pathway narrowed to maybe five feet wide with boulders and oak brush on both sides of the restricted valve. Once through it on your way up, it widened out enough on the top side to hold an army. If I could somehow lure them remaining Regulators to my mesa and get them started up the only trail to the top, and then get them situated on the top side of the thin opening, but not too far above it, I could have myself a duck shoot. They'd have nowhere to run fast enough to escape my aim. That, and I could also kick loose a bunch of big rocks down on them just to complicate matters even more.

My plan counted on them Regulators staying atop their horses as they made their way up the steep, rocky trail. If my estimation of these hired gunmen ran true, they were too damned lazy to get down off their mounts to do much walking. They liked doing their dirty business from the saddle while riding in large groups — typical cowards.

As I thought over the plan a little deeper, I envisioned killing the men and horses in the rear first, sending the bunch of them ass over end down the steep rocky slope and maybe clogging up the valve so no one could retreat back down the mesa. That way, there would be nowhere for them Regulators to go but up, and I would be hidden up there just waiting on them. Clogging that valve and offering them no retreat was the scenario to push for.

I walked down to that area of the trail and surveyed it real good. I took a look at the thin eyebrow of an opening in the trail and determined it could be stopped up with no problem if my shooting was good enough. There were maybe ten good size rocks and a few small boulders just waiting to be dislodged for a good roll down toward the narrow opening, hopefully taking out men and horses as they tumbled along. There was also good concealment for me behind any number of large rocks in between my firing and rock rolling. I sat there on that slope and pondered it over thorough-like and decided I was going to try it that very day, no waiting around. I figured to keep the action going against them Regulators without too many lulls. Keep them off guard that way.

If my plan worked the way I wanted, that valve would be clogged up with men and horses when the smoke cleared. I would have to find a passageway around that opening to make my own way down to the base when I had finished the job. I looked around awhile and eventually found a narrow crevice where a man and even a horse could squeeze through if needs must. The slit was much narrower than the narrow valve on the main trail.

I determined the easiest way to get them to my mesa was to start a small fire and allow the eagle eyes in their ranks to spot the smoke. Any outfit worth its salt would have men scanning the horizon on all sides, regular-like. I figured on a small fire because I didn't want my intentions to be too obvious. Wanted to make it look like I was trying just a quick, small fire for coffee or some such.

When I got back up to the mesa-top I started a small fire forthwith. Went against my grain to indulge in behavior that gave away my location, but that's just exactly what I wanted to do. I kept the fire going for about fifteen minutes and then poured a little water on it to make it smolder for a bit.

Then I went over to my favorite little spot in the rocks on the south side of the mesa and starting scanning the vastness of all that mesa country in that direction. I doubt ninety minutes had passed before I saw the dust of a sizeable group of riders. Soon, the riders came into view. It was a group of maybe twenty-five men and they were riding straight toward my location. It was my Regulators, for sure. "Frank," I told myself, "you shore enough bit off a chunk right here. You better hope your plan works or else your bones will lay here bleaching in this mesa country for a hundred years to come."

The sight of those twenty-five riders gave me to know I had thinned out quite a few of them with my work of the previous two nights. Must have killed and injured quite a few of them to get their numbers down to such a degree, and that gave me reason to be proud.

The hair on the back of my neck started standing and my heart went to beating as those Regulators rode in ever closer to my mesa. I figured my plan was sound but that didn't keep me from feeling the exhilaration of the moment.

They rode close to the base of the mesa and began looking for a trail up. I knew they would have to look for a spell before they found the only route to the top. Still, I scurried down to the top of the trail and situated myself behind a rock I had already chosen beforehand. I sat hidden there for maybe thirty minutes before hearing the sound of hooves against rocks below me. That gave me to know they had found the trail and were ambling their way toward me. "Alright, you sonsabitches," I whispered to myself, "come on up here and get some."

Of a sudden, a rider emerges through the valve and continues upward. A passel of riders follow him through and soon a group of twenty or more stand congregated there as if waiting on more riders to join them. Just like I had expected, every one of them stayed atop their mounts. I gave thought to opening fire about then but told myself to wait for each and every one of them Regulators to come into view. Sure enough, the last three riders through the valve were Doyle Campsey, Tulsa Tom and some blonde haired fellow I didn't recognize who rode drag.

I watched them all closely, and saw that Tulsa Tom was surveying the layout with some interest. Pretty soon, he got excited-like, started motioning nervously to Doyle and it was like I was reading his mind. Something told me Tulsa Tom realized the trap they had just rode into and was telling Doyle they should get out of there, muy pronto.

But I wasn't about to let them do anything of the sort.

I ups with rifle and shot the man closest to the valve — the blonde haired rider — out of the saddle and onto the ground in the narrow opening. His horse reared and fell over backwards on top of him. The horse must have injured a leg in the fall because it remained there on top of its former rider in a position that clogged up their one and only escape valve just as pretty as could be.

It was a beautiful sight.

Quick-like, I sat back down behind my rock, placed both feet squarely against its backside, pushed firm and hard, and sent it tumbling down toward them Regulators. The whole scene was one of great commotion. That big rock knocked loose a bunch of others on the way down and pretty soon it was an avalanche of stones large and small busting into them Regulators. Of a sudden, I stood up with rifle and commenced finishing off every Regulator I could. Downed men and horses soon lay piled in the area that would otherwise have been their exit. The scene down there was one of dead and injured men and horses what had fallen backwards into a squirming heap, a great writhing pile what blocked their getaway! I couldn't tell what had fallen to my rifle fire or to the cascade of tumbling rocks and horses. It was a beautiful scene of dead, dying, injured and screaming Regulators. Only a few men stood upright when the smoke and dust cleared. Two of those men were Doyle Campsey and Tulsa Tom, both dirty and bloody from all the action that led to the pileup of men, horses and rocks right by them. I yelled down to them.

"How'd ya like that? You all look like you've been horse-thrown and stirrup-drug! You sonsabitches!"

Ol' Doyle Campsey was use to being high and mighty and didn't like being talked to in such a manner.

"You're mine, Eaton! Right here, right now! C'mon. Just you and me!"

"Oh good. Face-to-face is just my game! Tell Tulsa and whoever else down there to sit this one out for us. You got this comin'."

I was still breathing heavy from all the previous action, and my heart was still pounding from the excitement of the fracas, but I walked down and stood within forty-five feet of Doyle with my drawing hands at the ready.

"I've done ventilated your brother and a passel of them Ferbers. Soon as I'm done with you I'm gonna take care of your other brother, Wyley. You make your move first, Doyle, just like the rest of them did."

Doyle's face was full of hate and rage, and both his hands were sort of cupped above his pistol grips.

"C'mon Doyle, your guts turn to fiddle strings? I'll let yours be the first rattle out of the box. Dig for it!"

Doyle's face grimaced and tightened as he went for his sidearms. His body took two pieces of lead and then crumpled to the ground in the same instant. His face showed shock as he lay there taking his last breath. Once I was certain Doyle was a thing of the past, I looked over to the few remaining men standing in the midst of the gunsmoke.

"Alright, you sonsabitches! Any of ya want a place at the table? I'm servin'."

The bunch of them were silent, so I walked over to the fellow I knew to be Tulsa Tom. He was standing by a solid looking black, one of the few Regulator mounts not injured or dead.

"Are you Tom Biscane, the one they call Tulsa Tom?"

"What if I am?"

"You ridin' that big black today?"

"Yeah, what of it, Eaton?"

"I'm appropriatin' him."

"I'll need that horse to help with those injured and dyin' men, and with those men already dead. What about them?"

"Bury 'em. Do the best you can with those that are gimped up. Where ya from, Tulsa?"

"Originally from south Texas."

"Go there. Now. I see you or any of these others ever again and I'll shoot you down like a damned mad dog, savvy?"

Tulsa was too dumbstruck to answer. He and the few remaining Regulators stood as if in a state of shock. Tulsa hesitated, squared up and gave me to know he considered facing me there for a second.

"Don't even think about it, Tulsa. You'd no sooner go to dig than I'd ventilate you and all the rest of your curs. Vamoose."

"You letting us live?"
"That's up to you."
"Why's Wyley Campsey so important to you? Was he leading the outfit what killed your pa?"
"No, he was taking orders from his brother, Shannon."
"So why waste the effort on him?"
"The job ain't done til I've settled with him."
"Eaton, you played hob, you son of a bitch."
"The Regulators were a sorry lot, Tulsa. Hook up with a real bunch. But first, get your belongings off that black. He's mine now."
"Whataya do next, Eaton?"
"Albuquerque. Wyley Campsey."
"You crazy? He's poison mean, lightning fast."
"Didn't say I was looking forward to it. Just got it to do."
"You just shot up and mangled a small army here, but Wyley won't be so easy."
"Like I said, I got it to do. Been on my mind for years."
"I don't get it."
"I was a kid of a boy. Maybe eight. I saw Wyley help murder my father, told me he'd kill me sooner or later."

"So you're gonna go find him just so's he can keep his promise? Leave it."

"Can't."

"He must be in your craw. If you find him and face him down then listen first to what I have to say."

"Go ahead."

"Wyley aims straight for the heart and finds his target every time. If you're facin' him head-on then shimmy to the right as you draw and hope that you only get winged."

"I'll remember that. You think I'm a dead man, don't you?"

"Look, I saw what you just did with Doyle. That was fast, damned fast. But that ain't gonna be enough against Wyley. Back out."

"Impossible. Every day of my life since my father was gunned down I've told myself what I had to do and have practiced toward it. It's a job what needs doin'."

"Well, there's another thing I haven't told ya. Wyley has him a couple of Mexican bodyguards these days. Faster than rattlesnakes. Killers. They're always close at hand. You might get one of them. Maybe two. But you ain't getting' three of them all to once."

For some reason, Tulsa felt it important to

tell me a few things that might save my life. I don't know why he did that. Maybe he liked me for some reason. Maybe he realized the Regulators were a no-account lot better off gone. Leastways, I walked up closer to him and shook his hand. His only words to me before I rode off on his big black were, "Nice knowin' ya."

I never saw Tulsa Tom or any of them other Regulators ever again. Counting Tom, my best guess is that I might have left five Regulators alive on that mesa. I didn't stop to count. All I know is that heap of men in the trail represented as beaten and broken a bunch of sonsabitches as you ever saw. And the few that might have recovered from their injuries were never going to be the same again.

Leastways, I led that big black through the narrow slit in the rocks, ambled over to the main trail and made my way down to the base. I needed to get to Albuquerque, muy pronto. That's where I would more than likely find Wyley Campsey, the man sixth and last on my list of distinguished gentlemen.

I also fancied the idea of seeing Adelita again. Her cards had said Albuquerque some years before, and she mentioned the old Spanish town when last we met.

Later, when I returned to the Indian Territory, I found folks wondering what had happened to all them Regulators what had terrorized the country hereabouts for years. Folks often talked about how the outlaw band had just seemed to vanish all to once. I didn't volunteer that they followed me out to that mesa country in eastern New Mexico where I sent most every damn one of them to an early grave. It was a good measure of man and horse murdering I done that day, and I wasn't exactly proud of it.

Many years later, when the Regulators of Indian Territory were just a distant memory, a line cabin cowboy found himself a pile of human and horse skeletons along a mesa trail out in New Mexico. We heard the news of that shortly after the Indian Territory became the state of Oklahoma. It was the talk of everyone hereabouts.

Again, I didn't volunteer a damned thing.

Didn't figure folks would believe me, anyhow.

15

My aim was to get to Albuquerque, muy pronto, finish my business there and wait for Adelita and her family to show up. I wouldn't leave that old Spanish burg without her.

After leaving Tulsa Tom and that pile of dead and injured Regulators about halfway up that mesa on the rocky trail, I immediately lit out to the westward. Over a course of days, I caught the Santa Fe Trail and took it first to Las Vegas and then to Santa Fe. From there, I took the trail to Albuquerque.

My first impression of that old Spanish town sticks with me to this day. With the Sandia Mountains serving as the backdrop, I rode into town and took in all the sights and sounds. The burg was a colorful mix of adobe buildings alongside brightly painted wooden storefronts with false fronts, impressive churches and assorted structures of native stone. I'll always remember the red chili ristras what hung in abundance and the sound of them Mexicans strumming on their guitars. Sometimes they would play that fandango music, fast and happy-like. Other times, they would hit slow, soft and sad licks that put one to pondering things like love, friendship, honor, courage and such-like. There was the clip-clopping of horse hooves, the squeaking wheels of passing wagons, and the piano playing and laughter coming from the assorted public houses.

And there were all kinds of people — Indian folks, cowboys, descendants of them early-day Spanish, and businessmen donning heavy mustaches and wearing derby style hats. There was just a hodge-podge of everything.

As I rode down Third Street, I thought of how I would look to all these folks. Here I was still carrying the war club and wearing those knee-high Comanche moccasins I took off that dead warrior back in mesa country. My hair had grown so long that I took to braiding it, and I couldn't remember the last time I shaved. I must have been a sight to see.

I hit town and looked straight away for the saloon and brothel district because that's where I would find Wyley Campsey. I soon found that area of town located along Third and Fourth streets between Copper and Tijeras.

As I was coming up Third Street on that big black, I ran into a couple of local badges. One was a tall, hawk-nosed, heavily mustached fellow smoking a thin cigar and wearing a crescent-shaped officer's badge. He looked to be in charge. The other fellow, shorter, wore a star.

The tall fellow stepped out in the street and motioned me to a halt.

"Hello, sir! You are quite the picture of the great American plainsman. New to Albuquerque?"

"Just rode in."

"No offense, but you look all in."

"Had myself a fracas back in mesa country northeast of here some days back."

"A fracas?"

"Finished up a little business you might say."

"What brings you to Albuquerque?"

"Somethin' of a private affair. Family business."

The lawman hesitated a little before speaking again, like he was sort of perambulating on what I had just said.

"I understand. Listen, if you're going to

be in town awhile might I suggest Molly Sinclair's place just down the way? She cooks up a good plate, has hot baths and soft beds."

"Thanks. Where does a man get outfitted with duds around here? I want to present myself well for a very special occasion."

"For the family business you mentioned?"

"Yes, that's right."

"Turn the corner here and follow the road until you get to Pemberton's. You won't miss it. But it's getting on to evening and he'll be closing soon."

"Then I had best be getting on my way. Obliged."

"You didn't give me your name."

"No, I didn't."

With that, I turned the nearby corner like the lawman had instructed, but I didn't go far. I stayed within earshot of those two lawmen just to eavesdrop a bit. I figured I might benefit to hear what they were saying.

I heard the short fellow speak up first.

"Just who and what the hell was that? He looks like he's been up the mountain and down the river."

"That, Thomas, is what you call the last of a breed, a man of the frontier, one beholden to no man. He gives no quarter to his prey and asks none in return. He gives the look of all that for one so young."

"Do you know him?"

"I know his type. And I like him. But watch him just the same. He didn't come to Albuquerque for no damned taffy pull."

All of that gave me to know those two would be watching me. Didn't matter to me none at all. I wasn't about to let anything or anybody stop me from doing what I went there to do.

It was getting on to evening, so I found Molly Sinclair's place forthwith, ate a good meal, shaved, bathed and then retired to a feather bed for the first time in what seemed like forever. The next morning I found Pemberton's store. There I bought new boots, spurs, jeans, gun holsters, belt, bandana, and a wide-brimmed black sombrero. I even found some fancy leather strips with silver conchos with which to tie off my long braids. I got all fancied up and felt like a new man. I also felt like finding Wyley Campsey, muy pronto.

I stepped out onto the boardwalk in front of Pemberton's and beheld a beautiful day. Church bells rang out even though it wasn't Sunday, and I determined it was as good a day as any to send Wyley Campsey to beyond the veil for good. But first I had to find him. I figured the gaming crowd was still asleep recuperating from the night before, so I walked around town for quite a spell, getting to know the place and allowing for the hours of the day to tick by and the saloon and brothel crowd to wake up.

The hours rolled by as I familiarized myself with the burg, and then the streets grew busier and the public houses filled with customers.

I strolled down the boardwalk and came to a public house called the Monarch, peeped in, and saw nothing of any interest. A few doors down, I took a look inside of a place filled with a strange smelling smoke — an opium den. There were two well-gunned Mexicans in there what looked like evil reincarnate. They were conducting business with the owner of the dive, a Chinese man. The three gazed back at me with a none too welcoming look on their faces, giving me to know I should proceed along apace, which I did.

I came to a place called Bremer's Saloon and saw nothing of any interest within. Lively piano music poured out of a place called the Cache Creek House some few doors down so I looked in on it. Again, nothing. Of a sudden, I turned around and found myself standing face-to-face with that tall officer who I met the day before.

"Officer, are you following me? Is there something I can do for you?"

"Well, yes, there is. You see, when a young man comes into town riding as good a mount as you have, with a Winchester under his leg and two guns strapped on, when he goes into every dance hall and saloon in town and doesn't take a drink or mix with any of the girls, he naturally invites a lot of curiosity."

"Fair enough. My name is Frank Eaton. My home is on Sand Creek in the Cooweescoowee District of the Cherokee Nation, Indian Territory. I'm a rider for the Cattlemen's Association and am in the line of duty. Now is there anything more?"

The lawman smiled from ear to ear.

"My name is Pat Garrett. I'm the sheriff hereabouts. Frank Eaton, I've heard of you and am glad to meet you."

I took him at his word on that and we shook hands.

"Frank, it's getting on to dinner. Let's go over to the Black Crow around the corner, the liveliest place in town, and get something to eat."

We took ourselves a table at the Black Crow and I immediately noticed that Garrett was right about it being a lively dive.

There were poker and faro tables throughout filled with players, scantily clad barroom girls prancing about with their bottoms bare for all to see, and equally sparsely clothed girls on stage dancing to the music of a live band with horns.

Garrett raised a hand and called for drinks. The bartender walked over to our table and I'll be damned if he wasn't the man sixth and last on my list of distinguished gentlemen — Wyley Campsey!

"What'll it be, Sheriff?"

"Two ryes."

Wyley left to fill the order and Garrett got right to his point of bringing me to dinner.

"Don't lie to me, Frank. I know you're after a man."

"Yes, you're right. I am. And, what's more, I've found him. It's that damed bartender, and I'm going to get him."

"Wait, son. He's a bad hombre! He has been in a lot of trouble, and he has two of the fastest gunmen in the country for his bodyguards."

"I don't care if he has the whole United States Army for bodyguards. He or I one will hear the cook call breakfast in hell tomorrow morning. Let's drink these drinks and then step out of here for a while.

Someplace quiet. I'll tell you why I am after him."

"Alright, Frank. I want to hear this."

Just a few minutes later, we found ourselves in the corner of a dimly lit dining area at Santiago's. After finishing dinner, we smoked cigarettes and drank rye as I told him why I sought Wyley Campsey.

"Wyley was running with a group what called itself the Regulators. His brother, Shannon, was the ringleader. They called my father to the door one night while thunder boomed and lightning shot from the sky."

"And they murdered him?"

"Shot him full of holes. I ran over and fell on father, crying and screaming. I was a kid of a boy. One of them took a whip to me."

"Was it Wyley who did that?"

"It was."

By this time, Garrett was just sitting there absorbing every bit of my story, genuinely interested, and I could tell it made his blood boil to hear what had happened to me and my family.

"Father had a good friend, a man named Mose Beamon. Mose came to me one day and told me that the curse of an old man would be on me all the days of my life if I didn't hunt these bastards down and kill them like low-life curs."

"Keep going, Frank."

I reached down and patted my sidearms.

"I spent the rest of my childhood days learning these guns. I eventually teamed up with Chris Adams, one of Judge Parker's men out of Fort Smith. He knew where to hunt them down. Knew their whereabouts."

"Where is this Adams now?"

"Regulators killed and mutilated him. Maybe not in that order. I done killed the men who done that to him."

"I've heard of these Regulators. Started out small in Kansas and then relocated to Indian Territory where they grew to a sizeable mob. They didn't like confines of law and order in Kansas so they moved down in the Nations where there is very little, if any, law."

"That's right, but they're not a mob no more. Finished them all over in that mesa country north and east of here."

"All of them? Is that the fracas you mentioned yesterday?"

"Yes, all of them. And, yes, in the very scrape I mentioned yesterday."

"Eaton, that is the damndest thing I've ever heard. I won't ask for the details."

"And I ain't volunteering any."

Garrett sort of grinned at that comment.

"Son, Wyley is trying to build the ranks of their gang right here in New Mexico. I can't have him do that. I've got my hands full with another bunch that goes by the same name — Regulators. But they aren't related to your bunch."

"I'm sure you don't need two such bands amongst you."

About then, I reached into my pocket and pulled out a badge and assorted papers. I showed it all to Garrett.

"This is my Deputy United States Marshal badge and commission. And this here is my letter from the Cattlemen's Association."

Garret took the items and looked them over.

"Sheriff, Wyley is also wanted for the murder of an officer in the town of Vian in the Cherokee Nation of the Indian Territory."

"This is something you had better not tackle alone. You know I cannot allow another killing if I can prevent it."

"You can't prevent this one and if you think you can, right now is as good a time to start as you will ever have."

"Hold on. You got me wrong. I only meant that you had better let me go over and try to arrest him."

"Oh, no, that man will never submit to an

arrest. He knows he'll go back to Fort Smith to dance a little strangulation jig for Judge Parker."

"You may be right, but how are you going to handle this one?"

"Easy enough. After we leave here, hang around a bit and when you see me ride over and tie my horse in front of the Black Crow you go uptown, and come back after the fireworks. It won't be long. I know he is fast, but I believe I'm faster."

"I don't know the caliber of those others you gunned down, but these road agents are lightning fast, especially Wyley's two Mexican bodyguards. I beg you, don't do it."

"If the bodyguards want to take chips in another man's game then I guess I will have to play them, that's all. I hope they don't, for they might lose and that would complicate matters for me with the local police."

"Don't worry about that. There will be no trouble on that score. The thing that worries me is that you have overplayed your hand. Three against one is a hard game and heavy odds."

"I've known I had this to do since I was a kid of a boy. I'll risk it and guess we'd better get busy."

With that, we both rose and I left money

on the table for the bill.

"Well, I like your nerve. You do for Wyley Campsey and you've cut the head off a growing serpent hereabouts. I wish you the best of luck."

"Thank you, sir, you sure are a man."

We both walked outside and Garrett disappeared. To where, I don't know. I walked back to the stable near Molly Sinclair's and saddled the black. I found and paid the liveryman who stayed in a ramshackle shack near the stable. I mounted the black and headed to the Black Crow where I tied reins about fifteen feet down from the front door of the establishment. I didn't want my mount in the line of fire in case shots were fired through that front doorway. I figured there was a very good chance I would need to high tail it out of these parts, muy pronto, after this affair was over. The last thing I needed was for my mount to take an errant round.

The crowd inside the Black Crow was a boisterous lot. From the sound of things inside, the atmosphere had gotten a lot livelier since Garrett and I left. I walked up to the batwing doors, peered over, and beheld a scene bawdy, loud and raucous. Barroom girls, breasts and bottoms bare, darted to and fro, delivering drinks and occasionally sitting on a willing lap. More mostly naked girls danced on stage to the music of a piano and several horn players.

Seemed like a damned shame to interfere with such a fun time inside. Fact, I rather wanted to join in, swallow a drink or two, play some cards and chitchat. That notion was overridden by my many years of preparing for this very moment. I had thought about this moment so many times and knew it had to be played out the hard way.

I parted the doors, walked inside, and I'll be damned if the first person I saw wasn't none other than the pretty buxom blonde from Southwest City, from the saloon where I had to shoot it out just to find out that John Ferber had been killed the night before. To be honest, seeing her again in New Mexico kind of threw me off guard, unlikely as it was. She was standing on stage next to some dancers and looking pretty as all get out, I had to admit.

Wyley, he was sitting at a table dealing cards. I wasted no time walking up to his table to face him. When I did, the entire place got quiet. I couldn't help but notice buxom blonde up there on stage pointing me out to the friends standing next to her. I could tell she was identifying me as the reason for the sudden hushed silence.

Leastways, all eyes were upon me, so I figured I had best do some explaining before I got down to business.

"Folks, I don't want the fun to end and I don't want to rattle anyone's hocks other than those of the man sitting here at this table dealing cards. And he's got it coming."

Wyley cast me a hard gaze. He wasn't happy.

"What's your problem? Who are you?"

"I guess you could say I'm something of a ventilation specialist, Wyley."

"A what? I said who the hell are you? And how do you know my name?"

"I am Frank Eaton and I ought to know you. You and your Regulators killed my father. Turn your wolf loose you sonsabitch."

Of a sudden, one of Wyley's bodyguards emerged from out of nowhere. He was one of the two well-armed Mexican gunmen I had seen in the opium den the day before. He stood right there next to Wyley, maybe three feet away.

Where was his friend, the second bodyguard?

Wyley looked up at me and smiled a skunk's grin.

"But what say you to these odds?"

"You're toting a busted flush, Wyley. I've

already done for Shannon, Doc, Jim and Jonce. Finished your low-life brother, Doyle, along the way. Also did for that small army of field mice what rode with him. You're next."

Wyley stood up from the table.

"That's right. I killed all of them Ferbers and them brothers of yours. See, you're the last of your mother's sons. What say you now?"

I was just trying to rile him so much that he couldn't think or shoot straight. It was a technique I liked.

"Damn it, Wyley! Why don't you throw down, you and that guard at the same time? Ya'lls can be the first rattle out of the box."

A few noticeable seconds passes by and nothing happens.

"C'mon Wyley, this is a very special occasion. On my list of distinguished gentlemen, you're sixth and last — dead last!"

About that time, both Wyley and his Mexican gunman went for their sidearms. I drew in the same instant and made sure to shimmy to the right just as Tulsa Tom had told me. I delivered two rounds into Wyley's chest and one right between the eyes of the bodyguard, but not before Wyley's round winged my left arm, rendering it useless. Moving to the right saved my life. I had told

Tulsa Tom and them few remaining Regulators on the side of that mesa that if I ever saw any of them again I would shoot on sight; but, truth be told, I figured I owed Tulsa Tom more than a drink for the advice he gave me.

Wyley crumples to the floor, falling over his chair and revealing Regulator boots decorated with those devil and death tarot cards. The dead Mexican gunmen was sprawled out close by.

A wild stampede breaks out among the bystanders but the shooting was seemingly over before most of them got to the door.

Now I gotta tell you a funny thing. I had just finished the job I had prepared so long for. I had finished off the last of the original six, had shot down the man who rode roughshod in my nightmares for many years, the man who took a whip to me after helping shoot father down like a damned mad dog so many years before. But I wasn't dancing for joy. No sir, I fell to my knees and the tears came pouring out of my eyes like a rainstorm. I guess I was just overcome by emotion, freed finally from what had been my life's grim purpose for as long as I could remember.

I looked up and beheld something vaguely familiar looking standing on the stage. I wiped the tears away to see better. It was the second Mexican gunman, Wyley's other bodyguard. He was in the opium den the day before with the other bodyguard I had just killed. He drew a pistol bead on me, and I saw the look of concentration on his sweaty, whiskered and unkempt face. I saw just the slightest smile begin to form on his face with his trigger finger at the ready. I saw his left eye close as he prepared to fire and then I heard the inevitable boom. The look on the gunman's face was one of confusion as he fell forward on the stage. Standing behind him, holding the small pistol with which she had just fired, was buxom blonde.

She moved the pistol up closer to her face and spoke to it like a person.

"Pa always said you'd come in handy one day."

Then she ran down the steps and over to me.

"You've been hit!"

"I'll live. Hey, didn't I see you not too long ago in Missouri?"

"Yes, in the saloon. You were looking for John Ferber. Had to shoot your way out."

"You're a long way from home, aren't you?"

"That wasn't home."

"I appreciate what you just did. Owe you."

I turned to get the hell out of there and ran smack dab into Sheriff Pat Garrett who had just come through the door from outside. He saw the blood on my left arm.

"How bad are you hit?"

"Not so bad but what I can ride if you will help me onto my black."

Garrett helped me onto my mount and, as he did, noticed that my left holster was empty.

"You've lost one of your guns. Here's another."

He placed a sidearm into my holster and then told me where I could ride for help with my arm.

"After you've ridden for a few miles you'll see a house off to your right. Go in there and tell 'em that I sent you. The Garcias will dress your wounds and keep you until you're ready to move on. They're friends of mine, good people."

I extended my thanks to Garrett, kicked the black, and began my way out of town. I hadn't got more than a hundred yards down the road until I ran into the three-vardo caravan of Adelita and her family on their way into town.

It was an eventful day of my life as I look back on it. I had just finished Wyley after spending my youth preparing for that very day. And then I ran into Adelita and her family just a few minutes afterward. Even though I knew she and her family would one day show up in Albuquerque, I was still surprised to see them just the day after I arrived in the burg myself. Leastways, right at that moment, I was some happy with the turn of events.

Sitting on top of the vardo was Adelita and her grandfather. Stevo trailed behind on his horse. I motioned the caravan to a halt.

"Adelita! It's me, Frank."

"What happened to you? You are bleeding!"

"Just got my last man, Adelita. It's finished."

About that time, Adelita's grandmother came around from the back of the lead vardo and cast a disapproving glare my way. In fact, she made the sign of the cross when first she realized who I was. Adelita stepped down from her perch and stood next to me.

"I'm ready to come with you, Adelita."

She gave me a serious look that made me feel real uncomfortable, and then she turned to her family.

"I can't. Not now."

"Whataya mean, you can't?"

"I'm married to Stevo."

By that time, Stevo had ridden up to the front of the caravan.

"I tried to tell you earlier, Frank. It's the way of our people."

"But we both knew we would see each other again in this very town. I thought you would wait."

Tears welled up in her eyes and started streaming down her face.

"I wanted to wait, but my family felt different."

"Does he love you?"

Adelita nodded a sort of yes. A weak yes, I thought at the time.

"Does he love you like I love you?"

By that time, the tears were rolling down her beautiful face and that gave me to know that I had lost a girl who loved me but who wasn't allowed to carry it out.

"Do you love him?"

"I will learn to."

With that, I looked over to Stevo, then to Adelita's grandparents, and then back to Adelita. They all gave me a look that made me know I had best face up to the reality of my great loss.

"My vendetta got in the way. I should have listened to you long ago, Adelita. Goodbye."

I kicked the black into a trot and we

headed east along the trail. I took one last look back to Adelita and she continued to cry her eyes out. Her tears told me she loved me, but the ring on her finger and the look on the faces of her family members told me I could never have her.

Facing up to that proved a hard gulch to cross.

When I rode up to the house Garrett told me about, I was met by a boy who looked to be about fourteen years of age. I told him that Garrett instructed me to drop by to get some hurts tied up.

The boy said that was just fine and to come on inside, that his mother would tend to my arm while he looked after my black.

"My father will return from town in just a bit and he will help, too," the boy said. "My God, man! You are bleeding like hell!"

It was right about then the father returned home.

"Hello, son," he said. "I see that you got here all right. Now, let's look at those wounds."

His wife brought water and bandages and he began dressing the wound.

"You're lucky as hell," he said. "I saw that fight and you sure handled your guns rapid. Garrett wanted to come along with me but he had to stay in town to look after things and pick up the pieces. The boys were drinking your health and some of them were getting noisy. And Wyley Campsey has friends in town and Garrett wanted to make sure none of them followed you."

The fellow looked at the gun that Pat had stuck in my holster to replace the one I had lost. It was a Colt forty-four sporting an eight-inch barrel and was very easy on the trigger end. A near perfect shooting iron, for a fact.

"Pat told me he gave you that gun there. You're mighty lucky. That's the gun Pat used when he killed Billy the Kid."

I looked at the gun with a little different perspective from then on and forever more. I didn't say as much to the fellow dressing my wound, but I figured it didn't bring Billy the Kid any luck at all.

I stayed with Pat Garrett's friend for close to a week and he tended to my wound every day. Then I hit the trail for home. I wanted to head to the Bar Triangle down on the Caney River and collect that reward money from Bill Knipe of the Cattlemen's Association. My heart was heavy with the knowledge that Adelita was out of my life forever, but the stars shone brightly in the sky and offered me their promise as I made my way for home.

And I wasn't forgetting that the great task of my life was finally finished. I had marked off the last man, Wyley Campsey, from my list of distinguished gentlemen.

16

The stone-faced old cowboy stopped talking and a long period of silence ensued as he stared into the bed of hot coals inside his blacksmith shop. He seemed lost in deep introspection and I took this to mean that he intended to divulge no more secrets that day. I remained quiet as he seemed to ponder the great questions of his life, long-asked queries for which he probably owned no answers. Something told me to respect the moment and this I did.

After a few moments, he turned his gaze from the fire and cast his eyes upon me.

"That's pretty much the gist of it, son. The long and the short of it. The good and the bad. I don't think I left out too much."

Naturally, I had a few follow-up questions and wanted desperately to engage him further.

"Mr. Eaton, can I ask you a question or two?"

"Call me Frank, son. Yes, you can ask all the questions you want. Don't know who else I would tell if not you."

So, for what seemed like the next hour, Frank "Pistol Pete" Eaton answered my many questions and told me even more stories as he did. I knew I was the luckiest boy in the United States of America to have heard firsthand the main story of his life and how he came to be regarded as a larger-than-life remnant from those lawless days many years before. The sound and cadence of his voice lives with me still.

He spoke of many things as he answered my questions, but the gist of the interview ran thus:

"What about Adelita? Did you ever see her again?"

"I saw her over and over again in my thoughts and dreams for years. Never saw her again in person. As much as losing her tore at my heart, a man has to somehow get on with his life. Same with me."

"Did you ever see any of those remaining Regulators again?"

"If you mean Tulsa Tom and those few others I left alive on the side of that mesa, no I didn't."

"Weren't you worried one of them might dry gulch you if they ever saw you again?"

"I had a premonition about Tulsa Tom and those others, you might say, and I figured they knew they'd been properly whipped and was ready to move on. Far as I know, they did. That Tulsa Tom, I figured he came to realize out there in that mesa country that he had been running with a sorry outfit and was ready to break away and make for a better life. It was just a gut feeling and I went with it."

"Did you feel bad about rolling those rocks and boulders down on them and spraying them with gun fire?"

"Well, another man's life don't make for a soft pillow at night. But, I figured when you're up against a small army what had tortured and killed your partner, what had murdered that Comanche warrior for no good reason, and what had taken pot shots at me as I made my way to Albuquerque, then, no sir, I felt no great amount of guilt. Not then. Not now. And I wasn't forgetting that this crowd was basically the same bunch of bastards what had shot down father like a mad cur."

"You mentioned those things called premonitions. You got them right before your father was killed and you got them again when you knew from out of nowhere them Regulators were following you out to New

Mexico. I've never heard of premonitions. Do you still get them?"

"Oh, I sure do. Mostly they're just little feelings I get at a moment's notice. Some people call them omens. I just know they are powerful hunches that tell me something is about to happen, and that something is probably not too damned pleasant. They come on me from out of nowhere and I get goose pimples on my arms, my heart goes to pounding hard, and the hair on the back stands up, and I know it's a forewarning. Like I told you before, the Good Lord outfits us with such, and that's why it's always important to trust your feelings about things and about people. It's the innate memory we seem to have of the experiences of our ancestors, people what lived hundreds and maybe thousands of years ago. In a way, them early folks is still warning us of bad things to come. Sometimes, I wonder if it's our ancestors who are also responsible for the epiphanies we sometimes get from seemingly out of nowhere."

"What's an epiphany?"

"Well, an epiphany is sort of like the opposite of a premonition. They both come to us from out of thin air, often as not, but a premonition usually indicates something bad about to happen while an epiphany is like a bright idea that can help us with a big problem or help get us out of a bad fix. You'll hear them preachers talking about how them Bible men got epiphanies."

"Kind of like when you got the idea of sneaking up on those Regulators at night and when you got the idea of how to trap them on that trail up to your mesa top?"

"That's exactly right."

"It must have been hard to let Bo loose out there in that mesa country when you were up against all those Regulators."

"You better know it was hard. Intentionally putting yourself afoot in any country whilst up against their like was risky business, but I knew I had it to do."

Frank Eaton then displayed a great smile and his eyes beamed with the memory of something that made them well up with tears of happiness. He shook his head and slapped a hand to his knee. He then removed his wide-brimmed hat and held it in his lap.

"I gotta tell you something, son."

"Yes, sir."

"Some years later, I saw Bo one more time."

The words brought a smile to my face. I lit up with excitement thinking about such a happy reunion.

"You did? How?"

"I sure loved that horse, my beautiful Paint! I was on a job for the Indian Territory Cattlemen's Association some years later. I was about a hundred miles south of that mesa country where I had the fracas with them Regulators.

"I looked off on the far horizon and spied a passel of wild mustangs just a-hellin' against the wind, wild and free as anything you ever saw. Beholding that bunch of horses brought a great feeling of happiness upon me, as the sight of beautiful creatures running free always does.

"They seemed to be making a beeline right in my direction so I stood on a rise of land and took in the action. Soon, the sound of their thundering hooves reached my ears and my heart took to beating against my chest in almost equal thundering booms. I loved seeing that band of horses charging along drinking the wind through their flared nostrils. It was more awe-inspiring than any band of winged Pegasus horses you might read about in a book.

"About that time, I thought I saw something familiar in that lead horse. It was the spotting pattern of white and dark coat colors on the leader that some reminded me of the pattern of white and dark on Bo.

You never forget such things about a horse that you rode for as many years as I rode Bo. The band was still a goodly distance from me but the familiar markings were interesting and brought a smile. As I think back on it these many years later, I know I must have been grinning from ear to ear.

"When the horses charged closer to me and I was able to get a good clear look at the leader my heart nearly burst with joy. That lead horse was Bo just as sure as I was standing there with my hair blowing in the wind, and he was leading him as beautiful a bunch of mares as you ever saw. They must have caught a whiff of my scent because they started slowing down and eventually they came to a halt about fifty or sixty yards out from me with Bo standing proudly in front.

"Bo was a handsome sight to behold standing there between me and his mares. He had come a long way, I thought at the time, from carrying a burden like me on his back for a period of years to now leading him a harem of beautiful gals and living wild and free as God intended.

"I whistled to him and his ears pricked up and he whinnied and snorted. He knew it was me and decided to come in a little closer. He stepped carefully to within maybe twenty feet of me and stopped short. I reached out my hand and called his name just as I use to call to him so many years before. He stomped the ground a little, whinnied and snorted some more and gave me an appraising look, sort of like he was saying, 'Yeah, I know it's you, but I ain't leaving these ladies and I ain't leaving my life out here where the plains meet the mountains just to let you hop on my back again. No, sir."

"I removed my hat and looked as best I could into Bo's eyes. I told him it sure was good to see him and that I hoped he would take good care of himself.

"Right about then, his mares started calling him back. He gave me one last look, kind of like he was saying goodbye, and then he turned to join them and off they stormed with Bo in the lead. It was a grand sight! He was free and that is what made the whole spectacle beautiful to behold. That same string of horses bunched together in a corral would be just another string of horses bunched together in a corral. They would be standing around swatting flies with their tails and waiting for someone to bring them their next meal. But, not my Bo and his band of mares! Creatures is always the most beautiful when they are free. Same with people.

"As they charged away, I watched them disappear on the opposite horizon from which they had come, and I said farewell to an old friend."

"Mr. Eaton?"

"Yes, son."

"You lost a lot, haven't you?"

"I ain't never looked at it that way. But, yes, I guess I have. Lost father. Lost Adelita. Lost Bo. And don't forget about Chris Adams."

"Sounds like you and Chris Adams disagreed about how to go after those Regulators, didn't you?"

"Sure we did. He respected law and order. So did I, at least when there was law and order around to be respected. I just had a gut feeling that the country hereabouts wasn't ready for his brand of law just yet. Then those sonsabitches got a hold of him."

"What did you do when you got back to the Indian Territory? I mean for a living?"

"I tried staying on with Judge Parker, working with some of his deputies, working to keep down cattle rustlers, whiskey peddlers and all other kinds of criminals. The country was overcome with the worst kind of outlaws in those days, and there was always work to do. I quit that after a while."

"Why did you quit?"

"That job didn't pay a man enough to feed his pony, let alone himself. Quit that and stepped up my work as a troubleshooter for the Cattlemen's Association. That paid good. Four hundred dollars a year, or one hundred dollars every three months. I was allowed to help any of the cattlemen belonging to the association who needed help. If one of them cattlemen came calling, I had to drop everything and answer the call. I received my regular pay and the cattlemen paid expenses."

"Did you ever work as a cowboy?"

"Sure did. Worked on some of the biggest and most famous spreads in the southwest. Rode for Clem Rogers down east of the Caney River for a spell after I returned to Indian Territory. Clem was Will Roger's father. I was working for him when I got orders to report to Captain Knipe of the Cattlemen's Association in 1882. I reported to Captain Knipe and he sent me out to the Muleshoe Outfit in Texas. Worked with that bunch as a cowboy while trying to break up a rustling outfit in their midst. I was a sort of an undercover cowboy. Did that a lot. Also worked for Captain Anson down in Texas on such a job. Even worked a little while for Colonel Charles Goodnight on his J A Ranch in Palo Duro. I was good friend with his nephew, Rolla.

"Rolla and I became the best of lifelong friends. I met him in 1882 when he was a tall rangy boy with sandy hair and honest blue-gray eyes. He lives west of here over to Guthrie where he farmed and ranched for a long time.

"Also performed as a cowboy for Pawnee Bill in his rodeo. In addition to his famous Pawnee Bill Wild West Show, Pawnee Bill had him a rodeo called the Old Town Rodeo located a half mile west of his mansion on highway 64. Started doing that for him in 1932. Me and Pawnee Bill became pretty good friends."

"Sir, I hear my father talking about the famous cattle trails. Did you ever help out on any cattle drives?"

"A time or two, son. Early in 1881, worked as a cowhand helping drive nearly five-thousand head of beef up the trail from north central Texas to the Osage Agency on Bird Creek. The Osage Agency stood where the town of Pawhuska, Oklahoma is now. Pawhuska is named after an Osage chief folks called Paw-Hiu-Skah, which means White Hair in English.

"We crossed the Trinity River the first day

on the trip north, caught the Chisholm Trail right below the Red River, crossed the Red River at Red River Station, and then crossed the Washita, the Canadian and North Canadian Rivers. We had trouble getting cattle out of quicksand in some spots and over some spots where it seemed like there was no river bottom at all. Son, always remember that these rivers here in Oklahoma are dotted with quicksand spots everywhere, and that means our nearby Cimarron. Always be careful. Leastways, we followed the Chisholm Trail for about twenty miles before veering off northeast through prime, beautiful country.

"We cut through the Sac and Fox Agency near the present-day town of Shawnee. We then made our way to the Arkansas River which was running swift and deep, so deep that we had to float our wagons across on cottonwood logs. I'm telling you, this was hard work, and a man was always glad to be done with it.

"On the last day, we swam the cattle across Soldier Creek and put them in the government pasture at the Osage Agency. The steers brought thirty dollars apiece and the cows eighteen to twenty dollars each. After we got paid, a bunch of us boys went to nearby Elgin, Kansas and painted her a deep crimson. And we deserved a good time after the work we'd put in with those cattle."

"Did you ever know any of the really famous outlaws in Indian Territory?"

"Knew Belle Starr for many years and stopped at her house often during those early days. I want to say it was about 1885 or so when I ran across her while riding across a prairie in the Cherokee Nation. She was wearing a large white Stetson hat and a long black riding skirt. She always rode in high style! People can say what they want about her but she sure enjoyed being around folks and loved having a good time. I always enjoyed her company.

"Leastways, we rode up to one another and shook hands. She was riding a pretty sorrel-red horse that day and I was admiring him. Belle said her horse was not only pretty but also fast. She said he could outrun any horse in all of the Indian Territory.

"I said, 'Belle, are you forgetting that I'm riding old Tex here?' "

"Tex was a buckskin I rode at the time and boy was he a fast one! I was some certain that he could outrun her pony.

"Belle answered that her horse could 'choke old Tex to death with forty feet of rope at four hundred yards.'

"To make a long story short, I bet Belle my Winchester against her belt gun, slicker and three blankets that Tex could leave her mount in the dust. So, we found ourselves a spot of ground about two hundred yards long without too much high grass. We threw out hats down to mark the stopping place. Then we rode across the prairie to what we figured to be about two hundred yards.

"I said 'Let's go!' and all I saw was Belle's long black skirt flying well behind her horse's tail and she outran me and Tex by a good ten feet of daylight!

"I pulled the Winchester from the scabbard and handed it to her, a model 1873 forty-four forty.

"Then Belle said she wanted the holster, to boot. 'Hold on,' I said. 'I didn't bet the holster!'

"She replied that I would look funny with a holster and no gun, and I agreed. I took it off and put the outfit on her saddle. She put the gun to use after that. That gun eventually wound up in the collection of Fred Sutton of Oklahoma City, marked as 'Belle Starr's Famous Winchester.' "

"Mr. Eaton, whatever happened to Belle Starr?"

"I remember the night that Belle was gunned down. I was at the same dance as her at a house near Younger Bend. There was a fellow at that dance by the name of Edgar Watson, and he was some sweet on Belle but she was not sweet on him. Belle and I were standing next to each other when Watson approached her and asked if he could escort her home. She didn't say anything. Just then, Belle and I hit the dance floor and it was my honor to have danced that last dance with her. After that dance, Watson approached Belle once again and asked if he could escort her home. She replied that she could get home just fine and had done so many times before. Watson looked some put out and I figured he thought I would be escorting her home, but I wasn't. Belle and I were just good friends.

"Leastways, Watson left the dance and rode out about two hundred yards to where Belle would have to cross the creek. After Belle left, she rode toward the creek, got there, and stopped to let her horse drink. That's when Watson shot her down from his hiding spot. We heard the shot and saw her horse after it had run back to the house.

"We got to the spot where she was shot and heard Watson's horse running off through the woods. We tracked him for over three weeks and for over one hundred miles. We caught up with him down in the eastern part of the Creek Nation. We took him alive after his horse was killed in the gun battle. Belle's friends hung Watson from a tree using her own lariat as a rope."

"Mr. Eaton, were you ever involved in any treasure hunts?"

"Well, son, you ever hear about our Wichita Mountains down in southern Oklahoma?"

"Yes, sir."

"Well, there are all kinds of treasure stories from those hills, and there is treasure buried there to this day in my opinion. I've been down there on many an occasion. Sometimes I was hunting men and other times I was hunting something else. I can tell you there are many stories of more than one treasure cache in those little mountains.

"Them Wichita Mountains hold the secrets to early-day Spanish treasure stories, Jesse James treasure stories, and quite a few others I'm privy to.

"I've heard folks hereabouts talk of a fellow named Fray Juan de Salas, the first Spaniard through there what established a temporary mission in the early 1600's. He was followed by Spanish gold seekers such as Captains Hernan Martin and Don Diego del Castillo years later."

"Mr. Eaton?"

"Yes, son?"

"You sure do know all the names of those early explorers. How did you come to know about all of that?"

"Like I said before, I've been down in that country many times, sometimes looking for men, but, more often than not, looking for treasure like so many others before me. I had a few pards what helped me on those trips and all I can say is we liked to do our research about those mountains before we set out. We read books, looked at old maps and memorized their every story and landmark. I have a drawer full of old Wichita Mountain treasure maps back to the house.

"One thing I can tell you is them early-day Spaniards what came through there were a bunch what loved hunting for treasure of any kind — gold, silver, precious stones, you name it. The thrill of the hunt for treasure runs through their veins. Our ancestors came to this new country looking for places to build up homes and towns, farms and ranches, but not so with them old Spaniards. No sir. They was looking for loot, and no Spaniard in his right mind would have passed up looking for such when they ran up on those Wichita Mountains.

"A long time ago, way back in the early

1600's, them Spanish men came exploring through there while on trading missions with the Wichita Indians. Them Wichita Indians made their home north of the Red River in the vicinity of the old, weather-worn mountains now bearing their name. Some of the original tales of treasure date to the time of the Spaniards who, some say, first mined the area for gold and silver.

"People have run across ancient Spanish ruins down there. To boot, there's a church down in San Antonio, Texas what goes by the name of San Fernando Cathedral what has early records of Spaniards from both San Antonio and Santa Fe who worked valuable mines in the Wichita Mountains in those early days.

"Folks have run across them old Spanish ruins, too. A bonafide Spanish settlement site, in fact. They have found old dugouts and timbers and caves that served as smelters where them Spaniards extracted the gold. That was found not too far from the town of Hobart. And there was an arrastra found not too many miles from the town of Meers, about two miles south of there, in fact. Folks have also found old mine shafts not far from the arrastra, so the shafts and the arrastra site are probably related."

"Sir?"

"Yes, son?"

"What's an arrastra?"

"Son, that's a primitive mill them early day treasure hunters used for grinding and pulverizing gold or silver ore.

"Of course, there's the story about the Jesse and Frank James, along with nine of their gang members who gallivanted down to Chihuahua in Old Mexico where they robbed that Mexican burro train. There's pretty good stories what account for about two million dollars buried in them Wichita Mountains from that little adventure.

"Them boys robbed that burro train around Christmas time in the year 1875. They arrived in the Wichita Mountains about three months later. They encountered one hell of a bad winter storm when they got there.

"While waiting out the storm, Jesse determined to cache the gold into a nearby ravine. Having caved in the sides of the ravine so as to cover up the treasure, the band burned the packsaddles and turned the burros loose.

"While waiting out the storm, Jesse used a horseshoe nail to scratch out a contract onto the side of a brass bucket found nearby. The contract, signed by each member of the band, bound them to silence concerning the location of the treasure, and it laid out some of the landmarks important in finding the loot.

"Before leaving the area, Jesse emptied two six-shooters into one nearby cottonwood tree and nailed a horseshoe onto another.

"After the turn of the century, the band's only two surviving members returned to the area in search of the cache — Cole Younger in 1903 and Frank James in 1907. I know that Frank James actually bought a 160-acre farm in the area after he returned in 1907.

"He was often seen riding through the mountains as if searching for something. He reportedly dug up other treasures of lesser amounts that had been buried during the gang's wild days, but he could never find the great gold cache buried in the ravine. After seven years of searching, Frank sold the farm and headed back from whence he came.

"Now, I'm going to tell you about another little treasure story that has to do with them Wichita Mountains, but don't want you repeating it until a few years go by. Is it a deal?"

"Yes, sir. I won't tell anyone about it for a long time."

"Good. You ever heard of the Lost Iron

Door Treasure?"

"No, sir, I surely haven't."

"Well, this story is about an outlaw gang friendly with the Wild West's most famous female outlaw, my good friend, Belle Starr. I just told you about the horserace her and I had over in the Cherokee Nation that time."

"Yes, sir. And you mentioned being with her at that dance and helping hunt down the man who murdered her."

"That's right, son. What I'm about to tell you stays just between you and me for a long time.

"Back in the mid-1800's, these bandit friends of Belle's robbed a freight train transporting gold ingots bound for the Denver Mint. The gang pulled off the robbery without a hitch, but they worried that a speedy chase by federal agents could land them at the hanging gallows before they could spend a penny of the take.

"They decided to play it safe and hide the loot at once within a Wichita Mountain cave. Before leaving the scene of the robbery, they removed one of the train's iron doors. They used ropes to drag the door to the cave during their great escape run. After placing the ingots against a cave wall, the robbers wedged the iron door into place over the cave entrance and then covered it all over with rock and brush.

"To mark the spot, they hammered a railroad spike into an oak tree that stood one-hundred yards from their hidden gold stash.

"After hearing that the gold might be buried somewhere in the Wichitas, federal agents searched the mountains thoroughly but came up empty.

"A few months later, all members of the robber gang were killed in another train robbery attempt. The only other person who knew of the treasure's location was my friend, Belle. Well, me and Belle, along with a few other mutual friends of ours, had ourselves more than one discussion about the whereabouts of the gold. Belle said she wanted to leave it in the ground where it was and safeguard it against any hard times ahead.

"After Belle's untimely death, me and some of those friends of ours took a few trips down to the Wichitas to take a look around."

"Did you find where it was buried? Did you find the iron door that covered it up?"

"I'll just answer your question with another question, son."

"Yes, sir. What's that?"

"Did you ever think that the reason you don't hear about too many treasures being discovered is that the folks who found them don't want to report their findings to the public because that would mean paying taxes on it?"

"I guess I have never thought of that. Sir, whatever happened to that dance hall girl you called Buxom Blonde?"

The size of Frank's eyes seemed to have expanded to the size of silver dollars and he stayed quiet for a noticeable few moments.

"Well, I didn't volunteer this to you before, but she followed me out to the house of Pat Garrett's friend and helped him look after me."

"Did you ever see her again after you got better?"

The old man hesitated again, only to break his silence after a few awkward moments.

"Well, you see, her and I sort of rode in cahoots for quite a spell after that."

"Doing what?"

The old gunfighter cleared his throat before answering.

"Her name was Clara Alexander and she was originally from Baton Rouge, Louisiana. Her and I embarked on a series of adventures that took us from Arizona to New

Orleans and from Galveston to all across the Rocky Mountains."

"Doing what?"

"Well, son, do you remember when I told you that I get certain premonitions, those forshadowings about things from time to time?"

"Yes, sir."

"Right now, I'm getting a pretty good forshadowing that your mother is looking for you down to the mercantile."

To be sure, I had completely lost track of the time that had elapsed as the old gunfighter, lawman and cowboy recounted his story to me. I didn't know it then, but I later realized that his stories about him and the buxom blonde Clara Alexander must have been too hot for my young ears to handle.

"Mr. Eaton, thank you for telling me of your adventures. I've never heard stories like yours before."

The old man extended his hand to mine and shook it firmly.

"I've sure enjoyed telling you about my past, son. And it's a pleasure to meet you. I've told you about some things that I haven't told anyone else."

"You want I shouldn't repeat any of it, sir?"

"Son like I told you before, I'll soon be

traipsing with those beyond the veil, and I won't be around to care one way or another. You repeat what you're of a mind to, but hold off a while on the treasure part."

As soon as I reached the door of his ramshackle blacksmith shop to leave, I realized I had one more question for the old man and turned back around to face him.

"Mr. Eaton?"

"Yes, son?"

"Did you say that you still have those nightmares?"

"You know, it's a funny thing about those pictures and sounds that come to me of a night. Yes, I still see those Regulators ride up to father's door and gun him down. I still see each of those six men bedecked in their fancy garb, and I still look up at Wyley Campsey after he has whipped me to hear him say he will kill me. And, yes, devil and death still dance on the walls of my nighttime world. But, son, these things are not nightmares to me now. They're just dreams and I ain't scared of them.

"These dreams are right in there with all the others, just an old man's hazy recollections of a time gone by, of a time no more. A time when buffalo roamed in the hundreds of thousands, when longhorns were pushed up the great trails, when Indians lived by the old ways, when wild mustangs rounded mesas with lightning speed, and when men lived and died by the gun.

"Son, I've enjoyed making camp with you. Always ride with your back straight and drink in the wind as it blows across your life's trail. May you always be blessed with good grass, firewood in abundance and fresh water at your sundown camp. And I mean that. So long, pard."

He escorted me to the door and then turned to find his seat by the fire once again. Before I closed the door behind me, I turned to get one last look at the grizzled storyteller. He gazed deep into the fire as if the flames ignited memories long lost. It seemed as if the exercise of recalling from his past had reopened long unanswered questions for him to ponder, paintings on long ago canvases for him to behold once again.

17

I then reunited with mother at the mercantile and we walked the few blocks to our home on Kenworthy Avenue. That evening, at the dinner table, a few minutes before my father arrived home from work, mother asked me about our trip to town.

"Tell me about your day. What did you do to entertain yourself while I was at the mercantile and the parlor?"

"Nothin' special."

"Someone told me they saw you down at that old man's blacksmith shop. Is that true?"

Not wanting to confirm or deny, no words were forthcoming.

"Jesse, I'm talking to you."

"It's true."

"I thought . . ."

"I know you told me to stay away from there, but I think you have Mr. Eaton all wrong."

"That's what your father tells me and I don't agree. That old man is a relic from a time gone by — a murdering time. I wish for you to never visit him again."

Just then, father came in from outside, walked into the dining room, seated himself next to me at the table and began conversing with mother.

"Did you two hear the news today?"

"Just that your son went into that blacksmith shop today and mingled with that old murdering outlaw."

"That's what I was about to tell you. Frank Eaton passed away today in that very blacksmith shop. They found him this afternoon. Took his body over to Stillwater, first to the hospital, then to the undertaker. Funeral is back here in Perkins this coming Saturday."

Mother froze, gathering her thoughts before speaking.

"He must've been ancient in years."

"He was ninety-seven years old."

"Jesse, I'm sorry about what I said about that old man."

Father, as he had done so many times before when mother criticized the old gunman, came to his defense once again.

"He came from a different time is all. He told great stories from those days, but some of us fellows wonder if he held back some of it."

"What do you mean?"

"Meaning, he came from a time when men sometimes had to answer the call as they found it — or die. Sometimes they did things we might think unbelievable today."

"I still don't know what you're getting at?"

"Frank was a genuine old time peace officer when the country hereabouts was wide open and lawless. All the old-timers talked about how Frank traveled to Albuquerque to settle with the last of those men who murdered his father shortly after the War Between the States."

"And?"

"That wily old fox had to outdo a gang of killers intent on not letting him get to Albuquerque. But he got there. He killed his last man. And then he lived among us here for years."

"All that town talk about Frank Eaton is true?"

"Some years after that affair in Albuquerque, the leftovers of such a gang were found out in eastern New Mexico, their bones bleaching under a scorching mesa land sun."

"Did old man Eaton do it?"

"I suspect that small army of killers caught up with him and that is exactly what he did.

He wouldn't admit to it, though."

"Why is that? For fear of going to prison?"

Father laughed.

"For fear folks wouldn't believe he defeated an army with nothing but his rifle, two six-shooters and his wits. Frank had grit and no back down in him. People are sure going to miss Frank and his stories. Many was the time people from around the country came to town to meet Frank and watch him show off his shooting skills and listen to his stories."

Then, father turned to face me.

"You got to go see him today, did you?"

"It's true. I did."

"I'm glad you did, son. You were the last to spend time with him, I reckon. I hope you visited with him for a good long time. What did you all talk about?"

"He told me lots of stories. He said he felt he didn't have too many days left. I got the feeling he wanted to say some things while he was able. Does that make sense?"

"Yes it does, son. If you're smart, you'll write down everything he told you while it's fresh in your mind. I suspect he might have opened up to you more than he ever had before to anyone."

"I will. I'll write down everything I can."

"That's good, son. We'll never see his like again."

A few days later, we found ourselves at the cemetery on the south side of town. Frank Eaton's casket lay next to the grave into which it was to be lowered. The scores of attendees were a mix of local citizenry — farmers and ranchers in their finest — and local and state dignitaries dressed in suits. I stood with my mother and father as we took in the scene. My mother noticed several well-dressed men standing next to the coffin and then she turned to father.

"Who are those men standing there?"

"That's the governor, Raymond Gary. That's the speaker of the Oklahoma House he's talking to. That other fellow is the president of Oklahoma A&M College, Oliver Willham."

"Why are they here?"

"I guess they know how important Frank Eaton was and still is to the people hereabouts. They know he helped clean up this country when it was nothing but a cauldron of cutthroats, killers and gut robbers."

"I guess. I know this is a bad time to ask the question, but do you really think all of his tales were true?"

Before father could answer, he and mother's attention turned to a mysterious dark-haired, olive-skinned elderly woman looking to be roughly the same age as Frank Eaton walking by the casket. She was accompanied by an elderly man with hair equally black and skin equally olive in tone. Around her neck, the woman wore a scarf trimmed in turquoise and red, with purple flowers against a bright orange background.

Just then, I remembered the part of Frank's story when he first met young Adelita and she read to him from the deck of tarot cards she kept wrapped in a scarf described as identical to the one around the elderly lady's neck. At once, I surely knew the elderly lady to be none other than Adelita, and the man by her side to be her husband, Stevo. Mother asked father if he knew this couple and he replied that he did not. I interjected that I knew the identity of the couple and then, with mother and father looking on in amazement, I walked over to them as they stood near the gravesite.

"Ma'am, you have never met me, but I know who you are."

She looked down at me, bemused.

"You do?"

"Is your name Adelita?"

My remark brought to her face a look of complete disbelief.

"You're Adelita, aren't you? Frank told

me all about you."

A tear rolled down her face as she digested my words.

"I am Adelita. What did Frank say about me?"

"Enough to know that you are part of his life."

"Whatever he told you, it's true."

The old woman stood motionless and quiet for a moment before continuing, recollecting memories from many years distant.

"I was part of his life when we were young . . ."

"I think maybe you were part of his life when he was old."

"Was he your grandfather?"

"No, just a friend."

"Whatever Frank told you is the truth. There was never a more honest man."

More tears streamed down her face. From around her neck, she removed the colorful scarf.

"Is that the same scarf you use to wrap and hold your cards?"

"Yes. He did tell you everything, didn't he? Would you like to have it?"

"Of course, I would. But he would like to have it more."

Adelita nodded in agreement. Then, accompanied by Stevo, she walked to Frank's coffin and draped the scarf over it.

"Goodbye, Frank."

Adelita's tears continued falling with Stevo placing his arms around her to comfort. She looked to her husband with kind eyes and a smile of appreciation. Just before they began to walk away from the gravesite to find a standing spot in the ever-growing crowd, Adelita walked over to me.

"I'm very glad I met you today. What is your name?"

"Jesse Stamper."

"Where do you live?"

"Right here in Perkins."

"I hope we see each other again. Jesse, I have a keepsake for you, one to help you remember Frank and I always."

Adelia reached into her purse and pulled out a stack of tarot cards.

"Ma'am, are those the same cards from many years ago."

"They are."

She fanned the cards out in a neat, face-down display.

"This is my gift to you. Pick one and keep it. Do not show it to me."

I ran my fingers over the cards and contemplated for a moment before taking hold of one. I turned the card over and cast my eyes upon it. I looked to Adelita and we exchanged smiles.

"Jesse, that was just to show you which one is your lucky card. Please take the rest of these cards and keep them. I want you to have them, and so would Frank."

Nearly one-thousand people attended Frank's funeral. In addition to the aforementioned dignitaries from the state capitol in Oklahoma City and from Oklahoma A&M College (now Oklahoma State University), were Rolla Goodnight, his closest friend, and Billy McGinty, one of Teddy Roosevelt's Rough Riders.

Frank's friend, Rev. A.G. McCowan, officiated the services and many true and kind words were spoken in the old gunman's favor. "He had a tough exterior, but was kind and tender hearted." "Children loved him and he adored them in return." "He loved to read poetry and often quoted Shakespeare, Plato and Aristotle."

A quote from Frank Eaton about himself was also recited:

"I know Saint Peter has me charged up pretty heavy, but unlike a mortal judge, he knows the innermost motive for every deed committed, whether good or evil, and I think He will not be too hard on a poor old cowboy who did his best as he saw it."

With his Cherokee Strip cowpuncher ribbon and badge pinned to his chest, Frank Eaton was lowered into the ground in the Perkins, Oklahoma Cemetery where he rests today. On his monument is written, "Cowboy, Scout, Indian Fighter, Deputy U.S. Marshall. One of a Vanished Era on the American Frontier."

His obituary appeared throughout the country — in the *New York Times, Newsweek Magazine,* the *Atlanta Journal-Constitution,* the *San Francisco Chronicle, The Cattleman,* the *1959 American People's Encyclopedia Yearbook* among others. To boot, his family received sympathy letters from as far away as Germany, Canada and Japan and was inundated with visitors at his home for many months following the funeral.

But Frank's story doesn't end there. In fact, it discharges booming fire and smoke to this day.

In 1923, a group of Oklahoma A&M students attended an Armistice Day Parade in Stillwater and noticed a colorfully bedecked cowboy named Frank Eaton astride his horse in the parade procession. The students decided on the spot he should replace the orange and black tiger then serving as the university mascot, since no such animals roamed the mountains and plains of Oklahoma as far as anyone knew. The university adopted the "Pistol Pete" likeness in 1958 and officially sanctioned him as a licensed symbol twenty-six years later in 1984, forever safeguarding at least the likeness of Frank "Pistol Pete" Eaton.

Among the nation's major colleges and universities, Oklahoma State University alone enjoys the distinction of possessing a mascot based on a single historical individual.

In 1997, the National Cowboy Hall of Fame and Western Heritage Center in Oklahoma City honored Frank posthumously by presenting him the prestigious Director's Award. Eaton's daughter and the president of Oklahoma State University accepted the award.

In the months and years after his funeral, I spoke with many people who had gained the friendship and confidence of Frank Eaton. They spoke of many other hair-raising adventures he had recounted down through the years, stories he omitted when he and I had sat by the fire of his blacksmith shop.

They spoke of a man who employed old world skills to live in modern times. In addition to working as a blacksmith, in probably one of the nation's last blacksmith shops, Frank also worked as a water well digger. He often used dynamite to break through layers of rock deep in the ground. Secured at the end of a rope, he often descended into a dark abyss, placed the dynamite in a strategic location, lit the fuse, and then quickly climbed the rope to daylight to escape the coming blast. There were many near misses. Folks said he laughed off each of these close encounters with death with a loud, hearty laugh.

I spoke with many of Frank's contemporaries who painted a picture of a deadly accurate pistolero and one-of-a-kind storyteller, showman and comedian nearly always dressed larger-than-life in his boots and wide-brimmed Stetson hat.

From a young age, Frank suffered loss of family and friends, lost love, and he faced it all with a stoic sense of duty and honor and responsibility. There seems little doubt he made a conscience decision to live out his later years living, loving and laughing to the hilt.

It was said he loved the company of people always, he adored children and he enjoyed hearing a good story or joke as much as he relished recounting them.

I have often wondered how often the gunman's mind rode the back trail to the night of his father's death, and if his humorous and over-the-top persona helped hide a scarred soul. Folks on the receiving end of Frank's jokes and tall tales may never have fathomed such a possibility, as such reflection struggles for a foothold amidst the fascination and wonderment generated by the old gunfighter's stories.

People who knew him spoke of the Victorian-era sense of propriety he employed when relating his many tales from those early days on the frontier. In the company of men, he cursed like a sailor, omitting nothing, however gruesome or shocking in the telling. When members of the fairer sex were around, he cleaned up the language and sometimes even modified the storylines to avoid offending delicate sensibilities.

To be sure, some modern-day cynics question the authenticity of Eaton's story of Old West bravado and revenge, but they have offered little or no revisionist history to counter it. For now, this fact places Eaton's story in stark contrast with scores of other more famous accounts from the early western frontier.

It's doubtful future historical findings will

subtract from the legend of Frank "Pistol Pete" Eaton.

It might do the opposite.

Like many another stone-faced yet polite survivor of that vanished era on the American frontier, Eaton may have taken to the grave more tales of blood and swash than he ever told while alive.

Not wanting to offend, the old timer likely held back the really good stuff.

ABOUT THE AUTHOR

David Althouse is a native of Oklahoma, having spent his formative years hunting, fishing, hiking, camping, and horseback riding throughout the state's Ouachita Mountain country. These days, David enjoys traveling across the American West, enjoying the people, places and history along the way.

"I enjoy hiking the old trails," David says, "scaling the slopes, traversing the mountains and mesas, and encountering all of the sights, sounds, and scents of the West. I feel at home in the places of which I write. I've had an appreciation for the written and spoken word for as far back as I can remember. I especially love the literature that speaks of the Western frontier — its history, fiction, characters, music, natural beauty, and romance."

A graduate of Oklahoma State University, David has worked in public affairs and journalism, and his writing has been published in magazines, newspapers and on websites. Most recently, David served eight years as senior feature writer for *Distinctly Oklahoma Magazine.*

The employees of Thorndike Press hope you have enjoyed this Large Print book. All our Thorndike, Wheeler, and Kennebec Large Print titles are designed for easy reading, and all our books are made to last. Other Thorndike Press Large Print books are available at your library, through selected bookstores, or directly from us.

For information about titles, please call:
(800) 223-1244

or visit our website at:
gale.com/thorndike

To share your comments, please write:
Publisher
Thorndike Press
10 Water St., Suite 310
Waterville, ME 04901